Harlequin Romances

OTHER
Harlequin Romances
by MARGARET MAYO

Many of these titles are available at you local bookseller,
or through the Harlequin Reader Service.

For a free catalogue listing all available Harlequin Romances,
send your name and address to:

HARLEQUIN READER SERVICE, ·
M.P.O. Box 707, Niagara Falls, N.Y. 14302
Canadian address: Stratford, Ontario, Canada N5A 6W4

or use coupon at back of books.

Perilous Waters

by

MARGARET MAYO

Harlequin Books

TORONTO • LONDON • NEW YORK • AMSTERDAM • SYDNEY • WINNIPEG

Original hardcover edition published in 1976
by Mills & Boon Limited

ISBN 0-373-02028-7

Harlequin edition published December 1976

Printed in Canada

CHAPTER ONE

TREVELYAN MANOR! It was difficult for Lenca to believe that less than a month ago she had been unaware of its existence. Now, as her car nosed round the final bend of the long, winding drive its mellow brickwork appeared to welcome her. The windows had turned to molten gold in the late evening sun and the gracious house stood proud and tall, basking in its radiance like a kitten before a fire.

It was easy to see why her grandfather loved his home. Who wouldn't enjoy living in this dignified Cornish manor? Built in the late seventeenth century on a headland a few miles west of Falmouth, it had captivated Lenca's heart the moment she saw it. The grey stone walls, crumbling and covered in ivy, stirred her imagination with vivid pictures of ancient Cornwall. Of rum-runners and nightriders, contraband and blackmail. Coming as she did from the heart of the industrial Midlands, the wide open spaces and the altogether different sounds and smells of this part of Cornwall all served to excite her emotions.

Deep down inside, though, Lenca still felt hurt. She could not even begin to understand why her mother had never mentioned her grandfather, why she had never brought her to see him. They had lived here once, when she was a baby, but then they had moved and it was as though it had never been. Only her grandfather could answer these questions now – questions Lenca had intended asking when she arrived yesterday. But she must wait, control her impatience. The last twenty-four hours had been so exhausting that all she wanted at the moment was a warm bath and the comfort of bed.

She drove round to the back of the building, admiring the roses which grew rampantly against the ageing stone; pausing as a black cat strolled unconcernedly in front of the car and then turning into the old coach-house which had been converted into garages. Locking up carefully, Lenca crossed the cobbled yard and went through a door which led into the kitchen. A warm, tantalizing smell of home-baked bread hung in the air, making her feel suddenly hungry. She looked round the lofty room, at the gleaming copper pans on the panelled walls and the Welsh dresser with the willow pattern plates, wondering whether to make herself a sandwich. Then, remembering that her grandfather had said Meg did not like anyone trespassing in what she considered her private domain, she decided to go in search of the housekeeper.

Daniel Trevelyan had been rushed away so quickly after her arrival that Lenca had not had time to familiarize herself with the layout of the house and now found herself lost in a maze of corridors with little idea of where she was going. It was a large house for an old man to live in alone, yet Lenca could understand his reluctance to give it up. It had been in the Trevelyan family for generations and as his sole remaining relative she would inherit it when her grandfather died. The thought was staggering. All this . . . She looked at the expensive tapestries, the furniture glowing from years of careful polishing. Meissen and Delft, exquisite glassware and silver, all displayed openly as though the owner was unaware of its value. It was too much to take in; so different from the semi-detached in which she had lived for most of her twenty years; her mother working hard, long hours to keep them in comfort.

Memories were painful, but all thoughts of her mother fled as she pushed open a door, recognizing instantly the room in which she had first met her grandfather. A smoky blue carpet was the perfect foil for the exotic colouring of Persian rugs, gracious chairs of differing periods blended harmoniously together and a beautiful table of gilt inlaid with tortoiseshell stood near the window. She had thought the house empty apart from Meg and herself and stopped instantly at the sight of a man lounging in a deep armchair, one leg strung nonchalantly over the side and a glass of her grandfather's best whisky in his hand.

He was in his early thirties, she imagined, with a craggy face topped by a mass of blond, curly hair. Making no attempt to rise he smiled broadly, even teeth gleaming whitely against weatherbeaten skin. 'I was beginning to think I had the house to myself. Do come in. Would you care for a drink?'

Ignoring his question, Lenca made no attempt to move. Who was this man? She had been under the impression that her grandfather lived alone. Was he an intruder who, knowing Daniel Trevelyan had been hospitalized, was taking advantage of the situation? Her heartbeats quickened and she eyed him warily. Apart from Meg – wherever she was – there was no one else in the house. It was an alarming situation. He looked harmless enough, but outward appearances could be deceptive. She clenched her fists, steeling herself to remain calm. Don't antagonize him, she thought; pretend there's nothing wrong. But she wouldn't go into the room, there was more chance of escape here if he should try any funny business.

'What's the matter?' he continued. 'Have I surprised you? Don't say Daniel didn't tell you about me? Where

7

is he, by the way? It's not like him to be absent when he knows I'm coming.'

So he knew her grandfather! That made things a little better – provided he was telling the truth. She couldn't be sure about that. She licked suddenly dry lips. 'Who are you? What are you doing here?'

He rose then. He was tall, taller than she had realized. Powerful shoulders strained his shirt seams, and rolled-up sleeves revealed lean, muscular arms. Brown, square-tipped fingers dwarfed the whisky tot, and Lenca sensed that it would take little pressure to crush it, if he felt so inclined. Involuntarily her hand fluttered to her neck. A pulse beat rapidly and she could almost feel his hands about her slender throat. She gave a half-cry and stifled it in a cough. She mustn't let him see that she was frightened.

'Quinn's the name, Devlyn Quinn. And you – let me see.' He stroked his chin thoughtfully. 'You must be some relation of the old man – there's no mistaking those eyes.' He looked into their violet depths and Lenca found herself staring into a pair of the bluest eyes she had ever seen. She wanted to turn away, but couldn't. It was as though she was hypnotized. 'Are you his granddaughter?' He sounded incredulous. 'There's a portrait in the gallery that could almost be you. I'll show you if you like.'

'N-no, thanks.' Lenca stepped hastily back. If he thought he was getting her upstairs he was mistaken! 'You haven't told me yet what you're doing here. Grandfather said nothing about you.'

'Ah, yes. Where *is* Daniel? You never said.'

For a moment she wondered whether she ought to tell him. He might not yet know that they were virtually alone. Where *was* the housekeeper? Why didn't she come? And then she realized that if he was genuine

8

he'd find out soon enough and wonder why she had withheld the information. 'He's in hospital. He collapsed last night shortly after I arrived. I've been there ever since.'

Immediately Devlyn Quinn looked concerned. 'Poor Daniel! I wish I'd known.' He crossed the room and poured himself another whisky which he drank in one long swallow. As though the news had been a shock to him, thought Lenca, still puzzled as to where he fitted into this household. 'How long is he likely to be in?'

Lenca shook her head. 'I have no idea. A few weeks, I should imagine.' Immediately the words were out she regretted them, but it was too late now to worry about the consequences. 'So if you want to see him there's no point in hanging around. Can I pass on a message?'

'I don't think so.' Devlyn Quinn's eyes twinkled. 'Except to say that I've arrived safely and not to worry. I expect Meg's got my room ready as usual.'

'Y-your room?' Lenca held on to the door jamb for support. He couldn't mean it. 'You're not staying here?'

He smiled. 'Don't look so shocked. I come for a few weeks every summer.'

'You mean that – you – and I – will be—?' It didn't bear thinking about. She suddenly wanted to turn and run. How could she live in the same house as this man about whom she knew nothing? She wasn't even sure that he was a friend of her grandfather's. If only there were someone she could ask – someone who could identify him.

'That's right,' he nodded, grinning now at her obvious discomfiture. 'Don't worry, I'm quite harmless. Meg will vouch for my character. Where is she, I wonder? It's not like her to desert the fort.'

9

At that moment, as if right on cue, a door slammed in the rear of the house and the sound of hurried footsteps were heard. Lenca looked round in relief. Meg, hot and flustered, wispy grey hair ruffled untidily and her arms full of parcels, came towards her. 'I'm sorry I wasn't here when you came back, Helenca,' she panted, 'I've been to get a few things for your grandfather and took the opportunity of calling in to see my sister. How is he, poor man? The place is like a morgue without him.'

Before Lenca could reply Devlyn Quinn brushed past her and wrapped his arms round the housekeeper's ample waist, swinging her round as easily as if she had been a child. 'Not any longer, my darling Meggie,' and he kissed her soundly on the cheek.

'Master Devlyn!' she squealed. 'Put me down or I'll drop the whisky!' He obeyed with alacrity and proceeded to take the parcels from her, placing them carefully on a table beside the door. 'I'd quite forgotten you were coming, what with the master being taken ill and everything. Oh, dear me! I must go and get your room ready. You've met Helenca, I see. I won't be a minute, then I'll get your supper.'

In a flurry she was gone, and Devlyn laughed easily. 'She never alters! You may as well have that drink now.' He turned and led the way back into the sitting room and Lenca had little option but to follow. She perched on the edge of a Queen Anne chair and quietly accepted the offered glass of sherry. Like the rest of the house the room was full of antiques and Lenca's eyes were drawn towards a beautiful carriage clock on the marble fireplace.

'Helenca. That's a pretty name.' Devlyn's voice reached her softly. He was back in the leather armchair he had vacated a few minutes earlier, watching her closely. 'After your grandmother, I presume?'

'I believe so, although I never knew her.' Lenca's reply was polite, but no more. He was clearly a firm friend of Meg's and presumably her grandfather, and she didn't know why, but she did not somehow trust this man. It might have been the circumstances of their meeting, she couldn't be sure, but there was an indefinable shadow of doubt in her mind. 'I prefer to be called Lenca.'

'Lenca it is, then.' He held his glass up to the light from the window and stared thoughtfully at the amber liquid. 'How is it I've never heard Daniel mention you? I rather thought he was the last of the Trevelyans.'

He seemed a trifle too curious for Lenca's peace of mind, but she shrugged and said lightly, 'I'm as mystified as you. Until my mother died a few weeks ago I didn't even know I had a grandfather.'

'Then your father must have been George Trevelyan?' He looked at her now. 'Daniel's mentioned him. Still seemed cut up about the whole affair, although it must have happened nearly twenty years ago. I didn't realize he'd any family.'

'I don't suppose my grandfather thought it any business of yours.' Lenca began to feel annoyed by this man's interest in their personal affairs. 'You still haven't told me why you're here?'

'My usual summer jaunt,' he said. 'I love Cornwall, don't you? Which is your favourite spot?'

'I've never been before,' admitted Lenca, realizing that once again he had adroitly changed the subject.

He looked at her astonished. 'It's incredible, with a family reputation like yours. But we'll soon remedy that. Name your place and I'll take you.'

'Thanks for the offer,' said Lenca coolly, 'but I have my own car. Anyway, until Grandfather's better I don't think I want to go far.'

'Suit yourself,' with a shrug. 'The offer's there if you want it.' He rose and stretched lazily. 'How about a stroll before supper?'

'No, thanks. I need a bath more than anything else.'

Half-way up the shallow flight of stairs Lenca turned and watched Devlyn Quinn as he crossed the hall. Anyone would think he owned the place, she thought with irrational ill humour as his long, easy strides covered the few yards to the door. She read arrogance in every line of his body. He was so sure of himself, so completely master of the situation, that she felt like screaming. Why, she did not know, except that he had aroused in her a fierce dislike.

Suddenly he looked up, grinning. 'Sure you won't change your mind?'

Furious with herself for being caught and hoping that he would not think she was interested in him, Lenca shook her head and, cheeks flaming, ran up the remaining steps, slowing down only when she heard the door close.

A row of portraits lined the gallery and she looked for the one which Devlyn had said was so like her. This must be her grandfather – there was no mistaking that aquiline nose and searching grey eyes – even though it had been painted many years ago. He reminded her very much of a photograph she had kept of her father and which was now tucked away in the bottom of her case.

And here beside him was Helen Trevelyan – her grandmother. It could indeed have been herself. Devlyn was right. Lenca moved uneasily; it was uncanny looking at such a close likeness. The older woman's hair was exactly the same shade of deep, rich brown. Subconsciously Lenca ran her fingers through her own short, boyish cut, at the same time admiring the thick ringlets falling down on to Helen's shoulders. She kept her own hair short in an effort to curb its tendency to curl, and could see now from where she had inherited this trait. Every feature was exactly the same – the deep violet eyes, the small tiptilted nose with the scattering of freckles, the wide lips, curved slightly as if repressing a smile.

Dragging herself away, Lenca looked at the rest of the paintings. Trevelyans through the ages – each one bearing a resemblance to the other, but none so close as her grandmother and herself. Inevitably her eyes were drawn back to this profile and although she knew it must be imagination she could have sworn the lips were smiling a shade more and that a gleam had appeared in the eyes. A chill swept through her and she hurried on in search of Meg. She was tired, that was all, pictures didn't change; her eyes were playing tricks.

Lenca awoke to a room bathed in morning sunshine and a nearly deafening chorus of birdsong. Yellow curtains swung gently in a soft breeze drifting through the open window. She could feel the air cool against her cheeks and flinging back the covers sprang lightly out of bed.

She felt refreshed this morning and smiled happily. One or two startled sparrows flew protestingly away from their resting place in the ivy as she pushed the window open even wider. The noise from these small creatures was really remarkable, she thought. Though most of the songsters were hidden from view the air was alive with sound. Lenca stood enthralled. At home it had been virtually impossible to hear the birds above the noise of the traffic which trundled through the town in a constant procession. Yet here the birds held precedence, proudly declaring their rights in the only way they knew.

When she went to bed last night it had been too dark to see from the window, but Lenca now discovered that her bedroom was situated at the side of the house. Hills and valleys in a mosaic of greens and golds unfolded before her, dotted here and there with farmsteads and cottages. The sun, a pale gold ball in the eastern sky, threw long shadows over the velvet lawns surrounding Trevelyan Manor and Lenca inhaled deeply, appreciatively. It was beautiful! Why had her mother kept away all these years? How could anyone not want to belong here?

The sound of a clock chiming in the lower regions of the house drew her out of her reverie. Was it really nine? Why hadn't Meg woken her? She slipped into a pink nylon housecoat which perfectly matched her nightdress and went in search of the bathroom. It was along this same corridor, but exactly where she could not remember. Meg had shown her last night, but this morning all the doors looked the same. She thrust open what she thought was the right one, but closed it again instantly upon realizing it was another bedroom – a man's room by the look of it. Not her grandfather's, she knew – he slept on the ground floor. So it must be Devlyn Quinn's! She had completely forgotten about him, but now memories of last night dimmed her pleasure.

He had returned after his walk and they had shared a meal in the – to Lenca at least – somewhat daunting dining-room. They had sat at a long table, and the meal Meg had lightly referred to as supper had turned out to be a three-course dinner. How she had accomplished it in the time Lenca could not imagine, and although she wouldn't have hurt the housekeeper's

14

feelings by telling her she would have preferred a sandwich in the cosy comfort of the sitting room. Instead they had been waited on as though they were royalty, and when Meg had eventually left them alone Devlyn Quinn had further irritated Lenca by telling her things about her grandfather which she would have sooner heard from the man himself. Eventually she had excused herself on the grounds of tiredness, a perfectly valid reason in the circumstances, yet she felt sure Devlyn knew it had been an excuse and had not taken kindly to her leaving him alone. No doubt his pride had been hurt, thought Lenca unkindly, not really caring what he thought about her. It was what she thought of him that was all-important, and that was easily decided. He was an arrogant, conceited, domineering male, a type she thoroughly detested.

Her hand still held the knob and acting on a sudden impulse she opened the door again and tiptoed into the room.

Tweed covers were pulled roughly across the bed and thick green curtains had been yanked untidily back by a man's impatient hand. The smell of pipe tobacco hung in the air, mingling with the faint tangy scent of aftershave lotion. Lenca sniffed approvingly at this typically masculine odour. The open wardrobe revealed an orderly row of suits and shirts. In fact the only thing out of place was an open book on the bedside table. Curiously Lenca picked it up and studied the cover – a collection of poems by Byron. Her fine eyebrows rose expressively – not at all what she had expected.

As she bent to replace the volume a piece of paper fell to the floor. Hoping it had not marked any particular place, Lenca retrieved the thin white sheet, noticing as she did so the words *Valancia* and *Manacles* scribbled across in sprawling black writing. They meant nothing to her and she pushed it carefully back between the pages, trusting to luck that Delvyn Quinn would not notice it had been moved – or if he did he would think Meg had done it while cleaning.

Guilty now for fear of being caught, Lenca left the room, closing the door quietly behind her. She had promised her grandfather she would be at the hospital early this morning. She must hurry now so as not to disappoint him.

Daniel Trevelyan sat up in bed and glanced pointedly at his watch when Lenca entered his private ward an hour or so later. She kissed him fondly before sitting down. 'Good morning, Grandfather. Did you think I wasn't coming? I'm afraid I overslept – must be this country air. How are you? You look much better today.'

'I am, girl, I am.' He spoke impatiently, as though his bed was already becoming irksome. 'If only those dratted nurses would leave me alone. Hope I'm not stuck here much longer.'

The grey eyes which had been so pale and lifeless when Lenca left him yesterday were now clear and bright. His cheeks a healthy pink and his still full head of almost white hair brushed tidily back. He patted Lenca's hand affectionately. 'Glad I've got you to visit me, I'd go half crazy otherwise. No one else has time to stop and chat. Take your coat off, girl. Make yourself at home.'

Lenca smiled indulgently. She was already used to the old man's brusque manner, but could imagine the nurses resenting his outspokenness.

'Trust Meg made you comfortable last night,' he continued in his deep, gruff voice, 'but she must have done, eh? or you wouldn't have overslept.'

'Yes, thank you, Grandfather. That reminds me, she sent you this. I don't know whether you ought to . . .' Her voice faded as he took the bottle of whisky, his eyes gleaming in pleasurable anticipation.

'Good old Meg! Knows I never miss my nightly tot. Put it in the locker, right at the back so the nurses won't find it.'

Lenca did as he asked, unable to spoil his childish delight by suggesting he obtain permission first. She then put the question that had been uppermost in her mind for most of the morning.

'There's a man at your house, Grandfather, says his name's Devlyn Quinn. I don't know whether—'

Daniel clapped a hand to his brow. 'Bless my soul! I'd forgotten he was due. Comes this time every year. You wouldn't know about him. You got on all right? But of course you did – he's a nice chap. I'm very fond of Devlyn.' Something in Lenca's expression must have told him that all was not as he had thought. 'What's the matter? You don't look very happy.'

'Devlyn and I didn't exactly see eye to eye,' admitted Lenca reluctantly.

Daniel's bushy brows shot up. 'You didn't! Why on earth not? What's he been doing?'

'Er – nothing. He was very polite and sociable.' Too sociable, she thought. He'd acted as though he owned the place. 'I'm afraid I was distrustful of him. You see, I had no idea who he was and when I found him drinking your best whisky I demanded to know what he was doing there.'

To Lenca's surprise the old man seemed to find the idea of his granddaughter not liking Devlyn Quinn extremely amusing and he roared with laughter. His face grew so red that she felt alarmed and placed a restraining hand on his arm.

'It's all right, m'dear,' dabbing at a tear in the corner of his eye. 'It's just that I can't imagine young Devlyn taking kindly to that sort of treatment.'

'Oh, no!' She couldn't let her grandfather misjudge his friend, even if she herself disliked him. 'He was a perfect gentleman. It was I who was not polite, I'm afraid. But what could you expect, Grandfather—' looking imploringly at him, 'when I found out I was sharing your house with a perfect stranger? He could have been a villain or a robber for all I knew. Meg wasn't there and I didn't know what to think.'

Daniel's laughter subsided, leaving only an amused twinkle in the piercing grey eyes and a quirk to his lips which he seemed to have difficulty in restraining. 'Don't get so distraught, Helenca. You'll find him a very likeable young man once you get to know him. He's been good to me. Let me see now, it must be five or six years since he first came here. He's a marine archaeologist. Did he tell you that? But no, he wouldn't,' as Lenca shook her head. 'Doesn't boast about himself. He's done some good work, both round the coasts of Britain and in the Med. Get him to tell you about it some time.' He shook his head slightly. 'Fascinating. He should be quite a wealthy young man by now. The treasure he's discovered is nobody's business.'

'And is that what he's doing in Cornwall, diving for sunken treasure? Or is he taking a holiday?' Lenca was by no means impressed by this account of Devlyn's activities. She still instinctively distrusted him and had no interest in what he did for a living.

'Bit of both, I think,' returned her grandfather. 'He does a fair amount of diving, but the weather's often against him. The Manacles are savage – you have to be

18

careful.'

The Manacles! One of the names on that piece of paper. But she still didn't know what her grandfather was talking about. 'I don't understand – what are the Manacles?'

'You don't know?' Daniel Trevelyan looked astonished. 'But of course you wouldn't. Unless your mother's mentioned them. Don't s'pose she would, though. Didn't like me, your mother. Must tell you about it some time. Now where was I? Oh yes, the Manacles. They're a group of rocks, my girl, about a mile out from the Lizard – you've heard of that, eh? I thought so. Well, the Manacles have the bloodiest record of any rocks around the coast of Britain. They've claimed thousands of ships. Thousands—' He appeared about to say something else, then changed his mind.

'I see,' said Lenca softly. 'And that's where Devlyn dives. Is he working on anything in particular at the moment?' thinking again of the piece of paper and curious as to whether the other word – Val – whatever it was – could be the name of a ship wrecked there.

'Don't think so,' replied Daniel, yet the way he averted his head made Lenca wonder whether he was hiding something. There seemed more to these two names than she had at first imagined.

It was not until later that evening that Lenca found out exactly what they did mean. She had returned from the hospital to find Devlyn still absent. Meg, when questioned, told her that he had been out since six that morning.

After a solitary dinner Lenca ventured into the library in search of some light reading. It was an impressive room. Books lined each wall from floor to ceiling. Leather-backed volumes nudged their newer neighbours. Paperbacks struggled for existence between heavy encyclopaedias. There appeared to be no order, yet she expected her grandfather knew exactly where to find any book he wanted.

There were books on every subject imaginable. He was obviously a man of wide interests – modern novels, the classics, Greek mythology, ancient history, to name but a few. Lenca eventually selected three modern novels which looked promising and took them over to one of the large leather-topped desks in the centre of the room.

A book lay there, already open, a well read one, judging by its worn condition. It was simply called *Shipwrecks* and a glance at the contents revealed that it covered disasters which had taken place around the coasts of Cornwall in the early nineteenth century. One name in particular stood out far clearer than the others: the *Valancia*. So she had been right! Eagerly Lenca turned the pages, inquisitive as to why it should be of interest to Devlyn Quinn.

There followed a graphic description of the tragedy of the sailing ship *Valancia*, but it was the name of the captain that caused Lenca's breath to catch in her throat – Sir Edward Trevelyan. Was he related? It was too much of a coincidence to suppose otherwise. She read on, eager now for details of what must be part of her family history.

The three-masted trading barque *Valancia*, under the captainship of Sir Edward Trevelyan, set sail from Falmouth harbour on March 24th, 1835, fully loaded with metal bars and small arms for Africa.

Unfortunately the *Valancia* never reached her destination. As she left harbour a sudden south-easterly wind took her off course. When the wind increased to gale force Sir Edward Trevelyan realized that they were heading straight for the Manacles. Despite all attempts to veer away from these dangerous rocks the *Valancia* struck broadside. Within seconds water spurted in and as she filled rapidly the deck tilted well to port. The crew scrambled clear of the now boiling waters, many climbing high up the masts in an effort to save their lives, but in vain. The *Valancia* sank lower and lower and as the Manacle Rocks reared up beside the ship she settled with only the tip of her mainmast showing above water.

Even though the captain knew his ship was doomed he shouted gallant orders to the last, and it is to his credit that no cries were heard from the crew. Each man went down as bravely as the *Valancia* itself. Only the bo'sun lived to tell his story. Almost dead with exposure; he was found many hours later by a search party who had seen their distress signal but had been unable to venture near the stricken ship until the turbulent seas had subsided. The bo'sun still clung to the tip of the mainmast when help came, and his recovery was remarkable in that within minutes of his rescue the *Valancia* disappeared completely from sight.

The story was told in far more detail. It went on to say that extensive salvage operations were carried out later that year, but although many of the small arms and metal bars were discovered the Captain's own personal possessions, which were believed to be of great value, had completely disappeared. When another search was instigated twelve months later by a group of private individuals, with an eye on the Captain's treasure, all trace of the *Valancia* had disappeared.

Lenca sat back in her chair, hardly able to believe all that she had read. If these accounts were true vast amounts of silver plate, jewellery and coins belonging to the Trevelyan family were still buried out there near the Manacles, waiting for some intrepid diver to discover them. It was like something out of a fairy story, and her eyes shone as she let her imagination run riot.

I wonder whether any more attempts have been made to relocate the *Valancia,* she thought. And then, almost in disgust, and unaware that she spoke the words out loud, 'I bet that's what Devlyn Quinn's after. I *knew* he was up to no good. Pretending to be a friend of my grandfather when all the time he's after information!'

'Are you talking about me?'

Lenca turned swiftly as Devlyn's voice sounded over her shoulder. She had been so engrossed in her reading that she had not heard him enter. Colour reddened her cheeks, but she stuck out her chin determinedly. 'I was. Can you deny that it's not true?'

He smiled tolerantly and dragging out a chair lifted one foot on to its red leather seat. Elbow on knee, chin cupped in his hand, he said, 'I might, if I knew what you were talking about.'

Lenca's eyes flashed and she patted the book. '*This* is what I'm referring to. Don't tell me it wasn't you who left it here?'

He glanced at the open pages. 'Fascinating reading, I agree, but then all shipwrecks are. I make my living out of them, in case you didn't know.'

'So Grandfather told me,' drily, 'but what about the *Valancia*? What do you know about her?'

'A little. All the information's there, as you've probably gathered. Unless you'd care to add to it?'

'Sorry to disappoint you,' drawled Lenca, unable to resist injecting a certain amount of sarcasm into her voice, 'but I've only just learned of it myself. I should imagine you've already found out as much as you can — from my grandfather?'

Devlyn straightened. His face became suddenly serious at Lenca's implication. 'What are you getting at? What's the old man been telling you?'

Realizing that if she was not careful she would give away the fact that she had been in his room Lenca shook her head. 'Grandfather's said nothing. It was quite by chance that I came across this account. If you hadn't left it out I should never have known.'

'How do you know I left it there?'

Lenca shrugged. 'It fits, that's all. Is that what you're after — the Trevelyan fortune? Haven't you made enough money without robbing an old man of his rightful inheritance?'

'Hey, hang on! Don't get carried away by that fertile imagination of yours. I haven't said I have any interest in the *Valancia*. You said it for me, remember?'

Lenca rose, feeling at a disadvantage with Devlyn towering above her, his face creased in sudden consternation. 'Then why are you here? What other reason have you for staying with my grandfather year after year? Don't tell me you like the place. Isn't it a trifle lonely for the likes of you?'

One fair eyebrow rose enquiringly. 'Are you trying to make me out a fortune-hunter? I may be dedicated to my work, but not at the expense of other people. We have a strong code of ethics among our profession, and they do not include taking what we cannot rightfully claim.' Lenca took a step backwards as he advanced towards her. 'There is also the law to be taken into consideration, in case you didn't know. Anything found on the sea bed has to be reported to the nearest Receiver of Wrecks, and only if the rightful owner doesn't make a claim within a year and a day does the finder reap any reward – even then it's only thirty per cent or thereabouts of the value put upon their finds. Naturally there are some unethical divers who never declare their discoveries, but on the whole we're a law-abiding lot.'

Hardly conscious that she had been holding her breath under this unexpected tirade, Lenca inhaled deeply and clung to the back of a chair for support. 'I didn't realize your job was so complicated.'

Devlyn whistled softly. 'Not many people do. They think it's a case of finders keepers. And now under a recent Bill for the Protection of Historic Wrecks a licence has to be obtained to work in any area round a wreck. Offences are punishable by unlimited fines.'

'I see,' breathed Lenca. 'So without permission you couldn't dive on the wreck of the *Valancia?*'

'Precisely,' and then, abruptly changing the subject, 'How is Daniel today? I presume you've been to see him?'

'Much better, thank you,' replied Lenca blandly. 'He's beginning to get crotchety already at having to stay in bed.'

Devlyn laughed. 'He would! He's a sprightly old man for all his seventy-odd years. He's never been inactive as long as I've known him. Did you tell him I was here?'

'Of course. He'd forgotten you were coming, but said he was sure we'd get on well together.'

'And so we will,' resolved Devlyn, an amused twinkle in his eyes, 'once you've got over your animosity. I've asked Meg for a tray of tea and sandwiches in the sitting room. How about joining me?'

He was obviously trying to meet her half-way and Lenca felt it would be boorish to refuse. On the surface, it seemed, she had no reason to suspect his motives, and though not altogether satisfied she agreed to his proposal. Only time would tell whether her own feelings were justified.

CHAPTER TWO

LENCA stood on the cliff top at Manacle Point looking out over the blue-green sea, alive with sparkling, dancing silver lights in the morning sunshine. White-capped waves beat gaily below and farther away the Manacle Rocks reared out of the shining water. Devlyn had told her some of their names last night – Shark's Fin, Maen Chynoweth and Maen Garrick, Maen Vor and Carn Du. He had also told her that Manacles was a corruption of Maen Eglos, the Cornish for Church Rocks. 'But their real secret,' he had said, 'is that far more lies beneath the water than ever shows. They're like the tip of an iceberg and just as strong.' She could see now what he meant and why they had earned their infamous reputation.

Bringing her grandfather's binoculars into focus on the rocks, Lenca saw a black rubber dinghy with an outboard motor moored between the points – a solitary diver keeping watch. Now and then an orange-hooded head bobbed to the surface, he would shout something to the man in the boat and then kick his fins into the air as he dived below once again.

Was Devlyn out there? she mused. She herself had risen early, unable to sleep, yet he had been out of the house even then and she could only presume that he was diving.

For all his assumed indifference in the *Valancia* Lenca felt sure he knew more about it than he cared to admit. He *must* be after the treasure. Why else would a young and undoubtedly attractive man like Devlyn befriend a person of her grandfather's age?

She recalled with clarity his statement that he had thought Daniel the last of the Trevelyans. Had he hoped to be included in his will? If so he must have been disappointed when she turned up, even though he had hidden his feelings admirably. He had skilfully changed the subject each time she tried to find out why he spent so much time at Trevelyan Manor, and now she could only believe that he was after some share of her grandfather's considerable estate – and what could be better than the fortune lying on the floor of the English Channel waiting only for discovery? His concern when he discovered that Daniel was ill must have been simply because he was worried about his share of whatever he found.

Retracing her steps to her shabby yet faithful grey Austin, Lenca headed back towards Trevelyan Manor. To reach the house she had to drive through the village of Porthoustock and impulsively she swung her car round on to the grey stone beach. The cliffs on either side were just visible from the upstairs windows of the Manor, but what she had not seen then were the huge quarry buildings. They spoilt the otherwise beautiful coastline and gave the whole area a sombre look even in the bright early morning sunshine.

Round the headland to her right she could see the first of the Manacles, their tips showing above water like the fins of giant sharks. And making its way towards them a boat with four divers clad in black rubber suits. As she watched one of the men lifted his hand and waved. He was too far away to identify, but it could only be one person, and Lenca turned away, wishing now that she had not come. She did not want Devlyn Quinn to think his affairs interested her. Without waiting to see more she hurried back to the car.

The road from the village wound steeply uphill and

it took all Lenca's concentration to negotiate it safely. Before coming to Cornwall she had never experienced such winding, narrow lanes and although she enjoyed their aesthetic charm, each time she met an oncoming vehicle her heart pounded violently. Fortunately in all her encounters the other person had reversed into one of the frequent passing places, allowing her to continue easily. She found the politeness and courtesy of the road users here so different from the aggressive horn-blaring drivers she had met in the towns where the whole pace of living seemed so much faster.

Now, as she turned into the drive, she felt again the magnetism of Trevelyan Manor and knew that it and the surrounding countryside had inextricably woven itself into her heart. Despite the aggravating Devlyn Quinn she was happy here and could not understand why her mother had moved to the Midlands never to return to this corner of England again. It was not long before she found out the answer to this question which had teased her ever since she arrived.

At the hospital her grandfather sat in a chair near to the window, and Lenca was amazed how quickly he had recovered. Only two days ago he had looked so poorly, yet here he was holding out a hand in greeting and smiling happily.

'Hello, Grandfather,' taking his hand and hugging him affectionately. 'You're looking very cheerful this morning – what's happened?'

'Good news, my girl. I'm going to be discharged in a few days.'

'That's wonderful! I'd never have believed you'd get well so quickly.'

He beckoned her to draw up a chair. 'You don't know me yet. Never had a day's illness in my life – till now. We-ell, only once, and you couldn't really count that. But never fear, I'll soon be as fit as ever, then I can welcome you properly. What do you think of Trevelyan Manor, eh?'

'It's beautiful, Grandfather.'

'Seen all over, have you? Most of the stuff's been in the family for generations. Priceless, some of it. What did you think of the set of silver plate bearing our coat of arms?'

Lenca shook her head. 'I've not seen that yet, nor all the house. Meg's always so busy and I don't like wandering round on my own.'

Daniel's brows knit together in a frown. 'Why ever not, girl? The place will be yours one day. Make yourself at home. Anyway, what's young Quinn been doing? He could show you round – knows the house as well as I do.'

I bet he does, thought Lenca, her grandfather's words confirming her earlier suspicions. He'd make sure he knew all there was of value. 'I'd rather not ask him,' she said primly, aware that the old man was waiting for her reply.

'What's the matter? Still feuding?'

'You could say that,' muttered Lenca. 'Though I don't see much of him. He's already out when I get up.'

Daniel nodded. 'Always been an early riser. Wouldn't lie in bed when the weather's fine. But in the evenings? He's at home then?'

Her grandfather seemed to know an awful lot about Devlyn's habits, she mused, and his voice held a certain affection for the younger man. Couldn't he see that Devlyn was only using him? That he was a mere pawn in the game he was playing? She shrugged. 'Not for dinner. At least, not last night.' Then recalling their meeting, 'By the way, I found a book in your library—'

'You'll find many books there, my girl,' a humorous twinkle creasing the corners of his kindly grey eyes.

'Yes, but this one was rather special – about the *Valancia*.' Was it imagination – or had she really seen a fleeting look of guilt cross her grandfather's face? Certainly there was no indication now of anything other than interest, but she was sure . . .

'And you want to know more about it, eh?'

Lenca nodded eagerly. 'Yes, please, Grandfather. Is Sir Edward Trevelyan one of our ancestors?' and as he nodded, 'I didn't know I belonged to such an exciting family.'

'Yes, Helenca. Let me see now, he must be your great-great-great-grandfather. Your mother didn't tell you about him?'

'Not a thing. She never mentioned the Trevelyans at all, nor encouraged any questions. I presumed that my father was the last of them.'

'And so he was,' agreed Daniel, 'except for yourself – and me, of course. There's plenty of life in the old dog yet.'

'I know there is,' placing a hand on his arm, 'and I'm going to help you enjoy it.'

'Bless you, child, you sound just like your grandmother. How I wish she could have seen you. You're so alike.' The old eyes were reminiscent as he gazed out of the window – alone for a while with his thoughts.

'I saw her portrait in the gallery,' said Lenca. 'It was like looking through a mirror.'

'Gave you a bit of a shock, eh? We must have you painted. Remind me when I get home – I know just the chap. Did me, you know. You've seen that one, I suppose?'

'I have indeed, and very handsome you look. But go on, Grandfather,' her eyes sparkling in anticipation, 'do tell me about Sir Edward. Was his treasure ever found?'

'What? Oh – it's a long story, m'dear. Best make yourself comfortable.'

The tale he told was virtually the same as Lenca had read except for a vivid account of Captain Trevelyan's private life. Daniel's brusque manner disappeared and he related his story with a faintly wistful expression in his eyes.

'Sir Edward's travels took him all over the world and he used to bring back priceless treasures for his wife to show how much he loved her. I imagine she would have preferred his company to trinkets, but he thought he was making her happy and so the presents continued to roll in.

'They had two children, Rachel and William, and apparently Sir Edward was looking forward to the day when his son could sail the high seas with him. Then suddenly both his wife and daughter contracted some obscure disease and died. All the money in the world couldn't help.'

'What a shame!' exclaimed Lenca. She could imagine how shocked Sir Edward must have been. 'What happened to William? Did his father take him with him?'

'Oh no. He was only eight at the time. Sir Edward hired a nannie to look after him; but not trusting a stranger in the house with all his treasure, he filled chest upon chest with the most valuable ones and took them with him on every trip.'

Lenca raised her brows. 'Sounds as though he'd got his sense of values mixed up. He'd trust his son to a stranger – but not his possessions. What type of a man was he?'

'That's anyone's guess.' He shrugged slightly. 'Not

that it did him any good, mind. When the *Valancia* struck the Manacles four years later his chests sank with it and as far as I know nothing's ever been found since.'

'And has no one tried?' Lenca could hardly believe that the valuables had been allowed to lie there undisturbed all these years.

Daniel threw up his hands. 'Goodness me, yes. Had a go myself in my younger days – but that's jumping the story. William tried when he was old enough, but had to give up. He lost a leg – and very nearly his life. You can begin to see how cruel the Manacles are. Not many divers will take the risk. You have to know the area and the tides like the back of your hand, and even then disaster can strike. The surface of the sea around them changes every few seconds. It suddenly opens like a giant, drooling mouth as it rips round some hidden rock; then pointed tongues of water swirl sharply together. Next moment all is still – but not for long—' Her grandfather had emphasized his words with eloquent movements of his hands, but now he shook his head. 'No – the Manacles are not to be taken lightly.'

Lenca shuddered. He had made it all sound so real – she could almost visualize the action of the creaming seas. Suddenly she felt a sharp stab of fear for Devlyn's safety. She did not stop to reason why. Did he know what could happen? But of course he did. He must be prepared, or he wouldn't venture out there. Yet greed reaped its own revenge. Look what had happened to Sir Edward.

After a lengthy silence in which her grandfather appeared deep in thought, he continued, 'My father, William's son, never even tried to find anything. Made no bones about the fact that he didn't like the sea. Cruel, he said it was, and never went near, even though it's less than a mile from the Manor. But he told us children about it. My brother Thomas and I were always asking him to tell us the story of Great-grandfather Edward. He was like a legend.' His face shadowed. 'Thomas drowned on the Manacles. I was thirteen at the time. I shall never forget my father's face when he was told. He forbade me ever to go near. The next year war broke out and in 1916 my father was killed. Sir Edward's treasure was pushed to the back of my mind until one day when I was about twenty, I saw that same book in the library – and without telling my mother I used to spend every fine week-end diving and searching. Then I met and married Helen. She didn't like me diving, but didn't try to stop me – not until the day I nearly lost my life.'

Lenca gasped and looked at her grandfather in concern.

'Yes. My leg got trapped beneath a boulder. I never found out what caused it to fall. Just as I thought my lungs were about to burst a co-diver saw my predicament and managed to free me. I was unconscious when we surfaced, but somehow he managed to revive me.'

As Daniel related his story a startling thought occurred to Lenca, becoming all the more disturbing with every passing minute. 'M-my father – what happened to him?' But she knew what the answer would be.

The old man stroked her hand. 'Yes, the Manacles took George too. Your mother blamed me.' He sighed deeply. 'She took you away and I never heard from her again. I knew where she lived, of course. I made it my business to find out; but I never tried to make contact – knew she wouldn't like it. Then when I found out she'd died I just had to get to know you.' He looked at her pleadingly. 'You don't mind? You don't resent me?'

33

Lenca's eyes were moist as she returned his gaze. 'Of course I don't. I love you, Grandfather, and I'm glad I've found you.'

'You don't blame me for what happened to your father?'

'How could I? It wasn't your fault. I'd probably dive there myself if I was a man.'

'Then thank the Lord you're not,' he said softly, pulling her close and burying his head in her hair. There had been a suspicious break in his voice and Lenca allowed herself to remain in his arms until he pulled himself together.

'What would happen now if the treasure was ever recovered? Would it belong to you as a direct descendent of Sir Edward – or would the finder be able to claim anything?' Lenca was thinking about her discussion with Devlyn last night and wondered whether her grandfather would now be classed as the owner or whether Devlyn, if he was lucky enough to find anything, would get a share.

Daniel settled back in his chair. 'There's something I've not yet told you, Helenca. Your great-great-great-grandfather left a will. It wasn't found until several years after he died, but in it was a clause to the effect that should his ship ever go down at sea any valuables that were subsequently discovered would belong to the finder – *if* he was a member of the family – otherwise they would become the property of the Crown, with a meagre ten per cent reward for the finder. You can see the way his mind worked. He wanted to make sure that every member of the family had the same love of the sea that he had. I don't think he ever really thought that anything would happen – or if he did, not in such a vicious area – or so near to his home.'

This additional information certainly put a different concept on the matter, decided Lenca. Devlyn must have hoped that as a result of his friendship with her grandfather he would receive more than the thirty per cent allowed him by law. He wouldn't know about the will; that he was obliged to hand over anything he found to the Crown, whether the owner was found or not, unless – unless her grandfather had already told him. She put the question hesitantly:

'Does – does Devlyn know about this will?'

He looked at her, eyes narrowed, then turned quickly away almost as if he was afraid to face her. 'Now why should he? What's it got to do with him?'

'He's diving out there. I suppose he has as much chance of finding anything as anyone else.' Lenca watched closely for her grandfather's reaction, but his carefully guarded expression gave nothing away.

'I reckon it's well nigh impossible to find anything now,' he sighed. 'The chests will probably have rotted away and their contents scattered over a wide area. The sea bed is constantly changing. What's visible one day could easily be hidden under several feet of sand the next.'

'I never realized,' said Lenca. 'I had visions of everything remaining exactly as it was when it sank.'

'A common storybook fallacy,' commented Daniel drily.

'Will you be very disappointed if the treasure's never found?' She had the impression that her grandfather had set his heart on seeing at least some of his ancestor's fortune.

He nodded. 'There's one piece of jewellery I would like to see. There's a photograph of it in one of my books. Remind me to show you some time. It's a gold ring set with rubies and a very fine emerald – the Trevelyan Emerald, it's called, and reputed to bring luck to whoever owns it. We've certainly had our share of misfortune since it was lost. I'd very much like to see you wearing it – but it's like searching for a needle in a haystack after all this time.'

'Never mind,' consoled Lenca. 'You tried – that's what counts.'

Her grandfather seemed tired now after so much talking and Lenca slipped quietly away. He had given her much to think about.

Instead of going straight home Lenca drove into Falmouth where she had coffee and sandwiches before spending the afternoon browsing round the shops and looking at the assortment of boats in the harbour. She had no real interest in the scene, however. Her grandfather's story was uppermost in her mind. He had made everything sound so real she could almost visualize Sir Edward setting out on that fateful voyage. Had his last thoughts been for his treasure so carefully collected over the years, or for his son waiting trustingly at home? No one could answer this question, and although Lenca would have liked to believe he was concerned for William what little she had learned of the man's nature made her think otherwise.

When she eventually arrived back at Trevelyan Manor she found a harassed Meg bustling along one of the upstairs corridors, her arms full of bed linen.

'What on earth's going on?' she enquired, following the housekeeper into a bedroom, and then as Meg proceeded to whip the dustcovers from the furniture, 'Have we got company?'

'Hmph!' She tossed her head. 'I'll say – and without a moment's notice.'

'Who is it? It's a bit inconsiderate to drop in like this.' Lenca helped fold the covers, stacking them

36

neatly on a chair near the door.

'Three friends of Master Devlyn's. Came with him just now – and he asked me so nicely I couldn't refuse. Seems like they've nowhere to stay.'

'Of all the nerve,' protested Lenca. 'The cheek of him! Didn't he think of the extra work? You've enough on your hands looking after a place this size without a bunch of untidy men to cater for as well.'

Meg was forced to smile at Lenca's indignant words. 'How'd you know they're untidy?'

'Aren't all men?' Then, remembering Devlyn's room, 'Well – most of them. I think it's a shame the way he's put on your good nature. You must let me help. You can't manage alone.'

Now it was the older woman's turn to take umbrage. 'Oh no. A spot of hard work never hurt anyone. You do enough racing around visiting that grandfather of yours. Keep him happy and I'll be happy too.'

'He should be coming home soon. He's made a re-markable recovery,' said Lenca.

Meg beamed. 'I knew he would. You can't keep that man down. It'll be nice to have him back.'

'And then you will need my help,' insisted Lenca. 'You can't look after an invalid as well as four men.'

'We'll see. Here, pass me those sheets, we'll soon get these beds made.'

Lenca smiled to herself. Meg was grateful for the help whether she admitted it or not.

Later as Lenca washed and changed in readiness for dinner she could not help but dwell on Devlyn's thoughtless attitude, and the more she speculated the more enraged she became. Had he done it on other occasions, she wondered, or was he taking advantage of her grandfather's absence? He knew there was only Meg to run the house. Admittedly most of the rooms

37

were shut off, with dust sheets shrouding the beautiful old furniture, but there was still plenty to do. It was really taking their friendship too far, she decided, putting down her hairbrush. He knew Meg wouldn't refuse.

She closed the door vehemently behind her as if to add emphasis to her feelings. Devlyn looked enquiringly out as she passed his room. He wore only trousers and held an electric shaver to his chin: 'Oh, it's you,' he said. 'I wondered what was going on.'

Her temper still at boiling point, Lenca spoke without thinking. 'What do you mean by springing extra guests on Meg? Don't you think she's got enough to do? This place takes all her time without more work.'

'Wow!' He pretended to stagger back. 'Hold on, give a chap a chance to explain.'

Lenca stepped forward and stood in the doorway, beginning to wonder whether she was speaking out of turn. After all, he had known Meg and her grandfather far longer than she had and probably knew where he stood with them. But there was no backing down now. She had started this thing and had to finish it.

'I asked Meg,' he continued. 'She said it would be all right. They're friends who've come to help me on this dive. They tried to get rooms in Porthoustock, but no go.'

'Of course Meg said she'd take them,' retaliated Lenca. 'She's too kind by far. But didn't you stop to think of the inconvenience?'

He scratched his head perplexedly. 'We'll be out all day. It's only a matter of breakfast and dinner—'

'With more than double quantities to prepare,' flashed Lenca, 'to say nothing of the extra laundry. You're like all men – see only your own side of the

38

bargain!'

Then suddenly he wasn't laughing any more. His blue eyes were serious and there was a tautness to his lips that Lenca would have been wary of had she known him better.

'Now look here,' he said. 'I've known Daniel Trevelyan longer than you — unfortunate though that may seem as far as you're concerned — and I also know that he wouldn't object to a few of my friends staying here. He's said as much in the past, only they've usually managed to find rooms in the village. If Meg needs extra help I'll see she gets it.'

'There's no need to bother; she hasn't complained. I'll help her myself if necessary. I just thought you ought to know how things stand.'

'And you took it upon yourself to play Lady of the Manor?' he mocked. 'Has Daniel deputized you to act for him?'

Hot colour swept Lenca's face and her fingers sought the wall behind. He was turning the whole affair into a farce. 'Grandfather hasn't said anything of the sort — but I am his sole heir, in case you'd forgotten.' She hadn't meant to say this. It made her sound as though she had only come to Trevelyan Manor in order to claim her inheritance — whereas in fact she had known nothing about it until she arrived and her grandfather had explained the position.

'Looks like you won't give me chance to forget,' he said harshly. 'Now if you don't mind I'd like to finish getting ready.'

Lenca gave him one last scathing glance and turned quickly away, only to bump headlong into another giant of a man, a wide grin almost splitting his face in two.

'Steady on! What's the hurry?' he said as she put out

her hands to stop herself. 'What have you been doing to her, Devlyn? I don't usually see women running away from you.'

Devlyn gave a tight-lipped smile. 'You'd better ask her yourself. If you're ready, Lenca will show you the dining-room. I'll see you later.' And without more ado he closed the door.

'Phew!' exclaimed the other man. 'I've never seen him in such a temper!'

Lenca sighed and started to walk along the corridor. 'I'm afraid I upset him,' then remembering her good manners she gave a bright smile. 'But this is no concern of yours. I'm Lenca Trevelyan, by the way, and you are—?'

'Kip Sterling,' he answered readily, holding out his hand and pumping her own vigorously. 'I couldn't help overhearing. If it's too much trouble, we'll go, only Devlyn said—'

'It's not that,' interrupted Lenca hastily, anxious to correct the impression Kip must have gained. 'Of course you're welcome. It's just Devlyn's way of doing things that annoys me.'

'He likes ordering people about, if that's what you mean,' agreed Kip. 'But his job's done that. He's always been in charge – even if he does disappear on occasions and leave the rest of us to it.' These last words were said so quietly that Lenca almost did not hear. But they could only mean one thing, of that she was sure.

Kip Sterling was as dark as Devlyn was fair. He towered well over six foot and made Lenca feel like a doll as she walked beside him. 'Have you known Devlyn long?' she asked as they neared the head of the stairs.

'A few years,' nodded Kip. 'We've worked together

on many dives. I've got to hand it to him, he certainly knows what he's about. It's not often he fails on anything he sets out to do.'

'What are you diving on now?' continued Lenca, waiting with bated breath for his reply. She didn't really expect him to say the *Valancia*, but it was just possible . . .

'A Dutch East Indiaman that went down in the early 1700s,' answered Kip. 'Devlyn found part of a ship's bell here last year and he's positive it belongs to the *Leeuw*, which struck the Manacles in 1721. He's organized this dive to see if we can find any more artefacts belonging to it. If so he'll instigate a full-scale salvage operation.'

'Sounds exciting,' said Lenca, slightly disappointed that he hadn't given the answer she wanted. Yet it was hardly likely Devlyn would broadcast his search for the *Valancia* if he wanted to reap any reward himself.

They reached the dining-room and as Kip opened the door Lenca heard the murmur of male voices which stopped abruptly as they entered. Standing by the window was a tall, thin man, wearing spectacles, and another much shorter person with a mop of curly red hair, both in their late twenties, she judged. They smiled hesitantly, as if unsure of their welcome, but relaxed as Kip advanced into the room.

'Alan, Trevor, this is Lenca Trevelyan. Lenca — Alan Jonsson.' The thin man with glasses held out his hand. 'And Trevor Brown.'

'Pleased to meet you,' said the smaller man, enclosing Lenca's hand in a vicelike grip.

'Lenca's looking after this place while her grandfather's in hospital,' continued Kip, 'so watch what you're doing or she'll be down on you like a ton of bricks.'

'Don't you believe him,' laughed Lenca. 'What he's trying to say is that we have only one woman to do everything, so if you could just make sure you don't cause too much extra work, I'd be grateful.'

'You needn't worry,' said Alan. 'We'll be as neat and tidy as two church mice.'

The idea of comparing these men with mice struck them all as very funny and the room was in an uproar when Devlyn entered a few minutes later. One look at his face told Lenca that he was not amused by the situation, and she could imagine his thoughts after the way she had gone on about their guests. Fortunately Meg followed close on his heels with the dinner trolley and in the procedure of seating themselves his displeasure went unnoticed by the rest of the party. Only Lenca was aware of his irritation, and the fact that he chose to sit next to her did nothing to help matters. On her other side sat Kip, with Alan and Trevor directly opposite.

Even with three extra guests the table stretched out empty on either side and Lenca sensed that the other men felt as overawed as she had herself the first time she had eaten here. She asked how they liked the house and about the work they were doing until gradually their tenseness eased and the men started talking naturally amongst themselves. Devlyn alone remained silent, despite the attempts of the others to draw him into their conversation.

Lenca helped herself to piping hot potatoes and buttered carrots from the silver dishes and turned her attention to Kip. If Devlyn was going to be awkward so too would she. 'Tell me about your work,' she said. 'What does it feel like to find something that you know was last touched by human hands hundreds of years ago?'

'It's difficult to explain,' Kip answered, spooning potatoes on to his own plate. 'It's awe-inspiring, I suppose – and exciting. It's like shaking hands with history. Look—' He opened his shirt to reveal what Lenca thought was a silver medallion on a length of chain. 'This is a Charles II crown. I oughtn't really to have drilled it like this, but it was the first coin I ever found and it's sort of symbolic.'

'It's beautiful,' breathed Lenca. Looking closer she could see the inscription 'REX. MAG. BR. FRA. ET. HIB. 1666' and a profile of the King resembling a Roman emperor complete with laureate head. 'Where did you find it?'

'Off the Isles of Scilly,' replied Kip. 'And this—' pulling a tissue-wrapped bundle from his trouser pocket, 'is what it looked like when I found it.'

Lenca gasped. These blackened, encrusted objects looked nothing like the one Kip wore round his neck. 'The sea does that?'

'Sure. Silver changes into black silver sulphide in salt water. An inexperienced diver looking for shiny silver coins would miss these altogether.'

'I should think so,' agreed Lenca. 'He wouldn't give them a second glance. How do you clean them?'

'Soak them in a solution of zinc and caustic soda,' he said, 'this reconverts the corrosion to metallic silver.'

Lenca pulled a wry face. 'It all sounds very technical. How about gold? Does that turn black as well?'

'Strangely enough, no. Nothing seems to touch gold. If you do find any gold coins they give you a welcome warning of their presence. Not that I've been so lucky.'

'You make it all sound very exciting,' said Lenca eagerly. 'How I wish I could dive.'

Another of Kip's ear-splitting grins. 'I'll teach you if you like. You can swim, I take it?'

'Like a fish,' laughed Lenca. 'I swam for my school when I was ten. Would you really?'

He nodded. 'Of course. It's easy. You'll pick it up in no time. We always carry spare gear so I should be able to kit you up okay.'

Lenca wriggled excitedly. 'When can I start?'

Her mind was already leaping ahead to the possibility of diving on the Manacles – perhaps even finding some of her ancestor's treasure. Then she chided herself for letting her imagination run away. If experienced divers had been unsuccessful what chance did she have? Beginner's luck, she argued back. It was worth a try.

Of course Kip had no idea of the reason behind her desire to learn to dive, except aroused interest in the sport, but it seemed someone else had. So engrossed had Lenca been in her conversation with Kip that she had almost forgotten about Devlyn sitting silently on her other side.

'Not at all if I have anything to do with it,' he interrupted harshly.

For a second Lenca wondered to whom he spoke, but when she lifted her head and saw that all eyes were on her, she knew. Even Alan and Trevor had stopped talking and watched with interest.

She forced herself to meet the steel blue of his eyes, the pupils contracted as to be almost invisible. 'I beg your pardon, are you talking to me?'

'I'm speaking to you both,' his eyes flickering to Kip and back again. 'I do not wish you to learn to dive.'

'I don't really see that it's any concern of yours,' retorted Lenca hotly, resenting his self-appointed role as her guardian. 'Kip's been kind enough to offer and I've accepted.'

'Then I blame you, Kip.' Devlyn transferred his at-

tention to his friend. 'The Manacles are far too dangerous for a novice. I thought you knew that.'

'Of course I do.' Kip shifted uncomfortably on his
chair. This was Devlyn his boss speaking, not Devlyn
his friend. 'But I wouldn't do anything silly. Credit me
with some sense.'

The blond man shook his head and sighed. 'Not
intentionally. But the Manacles are unpredictable. I've
dived them longer than you and I know. Far too many
people have lost their lives there, without anyone
taking unnecessary risks.'

'Okay, chief,' said Kip glumly, glancing apolo-
getically at Lenca. 'It's a shame, though, when the
lady's so keen.'

'Well, it's not okay with me!' Lenca almost shouted.
The two of them had been talking across her as though
she didn't exist and now it was her turn. 'I've made up
my mind to learn to dive, and if you won't let Kip
teach me I shall find someone else who will.' She had
no doubt in her mind as to Devlyn's reasons for not
wanting her to learn. He was afraid she might beat him
at his own game.

He looked at her now with ill-concealed impatience,
as one might look at a child who is persistently
naughty. 'In your grandfather's absence I feel it is
my duty to see that you don't come to any harm; but if
you still insist on this – this absurd notion of yours – I'll
teach you myself.'

CHAPTER THREE

SILENCE greeted Devlyn's words. Lenca was aware of Alan and Trevor waiting with bated breath for her reply and Kip at her side, fists clenched as if ready to wage war with his friend. They're all expecting me to refuse, she thought. Even Devlyn is sure I'll say no.

It wasn't that she wanted him to teach her. In fact the thought of learning to dive under his no doubt strict instruction was the last thing she desired. But it was as though some inner force took over and she found herself saying with a politeness she was far from feeling:

'Thank you. It's very kind of you to offer.'

'I can assure you my offer was not prompted by kindness,' he replied. 'Merely an endeavour to stop you coming to harm.'

'I like that!' put in Kip heatedly, but when Lenca nudged him he sank back into a gloomy silence. She did not enjoy seeing him hurt like his, but neither did she relish the idea of an argument between the two men.

Skilfully she changed the subject, but the evening had been spoilt and it was a relief when the meal ended and Devlyn excused himself. 'I'll give you your first lesson in the morning,' he called from the doorway. 'Be ready about nine.'

He was gone before Lenca could mention that she usually spent her day at the hospital. Never mind, she thought, I'll ring Grandfather. He'll be pleased to learn I'm spending time with Devlyn.

She chatted with the men for a while, but sensed that they were waiting for her too to go so that they could discuss and wonder on the friction between her and

Devlyn. She recalled Kip's remark that he had never seen a woman run away from Devlyn before, and wondered how many women friends he had. He was a very attractive man and she imagined him to be very popular. It was only with her that he seemed to go out of his way to be antagonistic. Not that she would like it any different, she hastily assured herself. Devlyn Quinn was not her type.

Lenca slept deeply and dreamlessly that night, until woken by her alarm at seven-thirty. One glance outside showed that the golden warmth of the last few days had gone. The hills lay wreathed in shadow; the sky was an indeterminate grey and a fine mist blew across her face as she looked through the open window. She shivered and shrugging into her housecoat made straight for the bathroom. Presumably Devlyn would still keep his promise. It couldn't make much difference in the sea whether the sun was shining or not. But here she was wrong.

Devlyn was already in the dining room when she went down, looking very dashing in a cream silk shirt and beige slacks. 'I'm afraid the lesson's off,' he said, after one glance at her excited face. 'The wind's getting stronger by the minute. No point in courting disaster.'

Lenca looked from him to the faces of Kip, Alan and Trevor. They looked equally gloomy. 'He's right,' ventured Alan. 'Even we can't go out today. Trust this to happen now!'

'Never mind,' said Devlyn. 'There's plenty to keep you occupied.'

'Like cleaning that stuff you've found?' grumbled Trevor good-naturedly. 'We don't object, but it's not the same.'

'You didn't tell me you'd already made some discoveries. Lenca looked eagerly at Devlyn.

'You didn't ask,' came the smooth reply. 'The arte-facts are in the cellar if you want to see them. Your grandfather's turned part of it over to me for a work-shop.'

This was something else about which Lenca knew nothing, but this time she wisely kept her own counsel. There was no point in knowingly entering into an argu-ment with Devlyn; but he certainly seemed to have a lot of his own way round here and she was not sure whether she liked it.

'I doubt if you'll find them interesting,' he con-tinued. 'A few pottery fragments, partially disinte-grated cannon balls, coins, an ormolu dagger hilt. Nothing conclusive.'

It was almost as though he didn't want her to see, thought Lenca; as though he had something to hide. This decision made her determined to go down and take a look for herself as soon as a suitable opportunity arose. Not when he was there, but when the house was empty, when she was sure of being undisturbed.

But Devlyn's next words took all thoughts of sunken treasure out of her mind.

'As we can't dive how would you like the day out with me?'

Lenca stared. She couldn't believe that she had heard him correctly. 'Out – with you?' she stammered at last.

'That's right,' smiling now. 'Is the idea so abhor-rent?'

No, she thought, it wasn't that, merely surprising. Whenever they met they argued, yet now he suggested spending a whole day together. It could be interest-ing, though. She might find out a lot more about this man who had so suddenly appeared in her life.

'Okay,' she said at last. 'I'll come. But I must be back

for six. Grandfather's expecting me then.'

'Fair deal,' he agreed, attacking his ham with relish. His head bent, he did not see the other men smiling, but Lenca did, and wondered whether she had given in too easily after their skirmish yesterday. She gave a mental shrug. Too late now to change her mind. The matter was settled so far as Devlyn was concerned. She could only hope that the day would not turn out to be a disaster.

Devlyn revved the engine and looked up impatiently as Lenca approached. She had suggested changing, but he said her blue denim trouser suit would do perfectly well. Even so it appeared she had not been quick enough. However, he jumped out and opened the door and Lenca eased herself into the opulent luxury of his white Alfa. I might have known he would own a car like this, she thought, looking round her appreciatively – cream leather upholstery, gleaming fittings, wireless, cassette player, bar; every conceivable luxury. They drew away and it was like floating on air. This is what money can do, she thought, recalling her own battered little car which made every bump in the road feel like a mountain.

'Comfortable?' he enquired, and as she nodded, 'Where would you like to go? Land's End? Dartmoor? The choice is yours. Anywhere you like.'

'I don't mind, really,' said Lenca, suddenly nervous. She was not used to him treating her so gently; almost as though he genuinely cared, which was ridiculous.

'Nowhere's too good in this weather, of course,' he said, 'but we'll try Land's End. We can always do Dartmoor another day.'

So he had further outings in view? Lenca was not so sure, but said nothing. Silence was the wisest course in a case like this.

He drove though the village of Porthoustock — very grey and still on this dismal late August morning — stopping a few miles later in the square at St. Keverne. Lenca looked at him enquiringly. He had hardly spoken during the journey and she wondered whether he was having second thoughts.

'Some of your ancestors are buried in the church-yard here. Would you care to see? Or wait until Daniel's well enough to bring you?'

'We'll go now,' said Lenca in sudden interest. It would help build up a clearer picture of the family she had so recently discovered.

She was very conscious of his nearness as together they climbed the steps and when his hand touched hers, simultaneously reaching out to open the iron gate, a tingling sensation ran through her arm which she was at a loss to understand. She put it down to animosity — there was nothing else it could be — yet this morning he was a different person. If only he was like this all the time I might even like him, she mused.

But all thoughts fled as they walked along the path skirting the church. The atmosphere had subtly changed. An all-pervading peace surrounded them. The church stood grey and solemn, its spire reaching up towards the shaded emptiness that was the sky. Huge clumps of hydrangea in varying hues grew close to its walls, and all around them the headstones; some old and some new; some scarcely legible, others startling in their clarity.

Silently Devlyn led her to a far corner. Here Lenca saw the names that before her grandfather's talk would have meant nothing. She stood for a few moments thinking about the tragedy of the Trevelyan family, until Devlyn caught her fingers. 'Come,' he said, 'time we were going.'

If she had looked up she would have seen the tenderness that softened his face, but so caught up was Lenca in the history of her family that she allowed herself to be led away without realizing that she held the hand of the man she disliked so much.

He stopped again after a few yards, indicating a white monument. 'This is where they buried the victims of the *Mohegan,* probably one of the most famous shipwrecks on the Manacles. She was a new passenger liner heading for New York and hit the Manacles almost at full speed. Over a hundred people drowned.' Lenca shivered and he put his arm protectively about her shoulders. 'Can't you see why I don't want you to dive there? It's too dangerous.'

She stiffened, all her earlier mistrust returning. 'Are you backing out? I've only to ask Kip. He'll teach me.'

'Of course I'm not backing out,' he sighed. 'It's just that you don't seem fully aware of the danger.'

Lenca moved a few steps away and faced him. 'Is that why you've brought me here?' she whispered fiercely. 'Not to show me where my relations are buried, but this—' pointing to the carved stone. 'Did you think it might deter me?'

'The thought never entered my head. I'd forgotten about it till now. I hoped it might interest you, that's all.'

He spoke sincerely and Lenca lowered her eyes under his steady gaze. There seemed no more to be said. If he was speaking the truth she had misjudged him. If so, she was sorry – but could she believe him? It was a difficult decision and one she did not intend making now.

'Let's go,' he said. 'Maybe it was a mistake bringing you here.'

She gave a half apologetic smile. He really was

trying hard to be nice today. It would be a pity to spoil it by allowing her own doubts to overshadow everything. There and then she determined to enjoy herself. Surely I can forget for a few hours what an unscrupulous character he is? she asked herself. It shouldn't be too hard.

Back in the car they sped along leafy lanes; the trees met overhead and the road, looking like a long, green tunnel, suddenly opened out on to wide, sweeping downs. A few farmsteads dotted the landscape. Heather and trees added interest to this flatter and, in Lenca's opinion, less attractive part of Cornwall, and then suddenly three gigantic dish-shaped objects came into sight, looking like something out of a science fiction film. Lenca's hand fluttered unconsciously to her throat. 'What's that?' The two words cut into their silence like an explosion and Devlyn laughed.

'It's Goonhilly Downs Earth Satellite Station. Like something from out of space, don't you think?' Red and white lights glowed in the semi-darkness caused by the swirling mist and as Devlyn slowed down so that they could take a closer look Lenca shuddered.

'It's eerie,' she said. 'Drive on. I don't like it.' He seemed amused, but obediently put down his foot and the Alfa gathered up speed as they headed towards Penzance and Land's End.

Lenca was disappointed in Land's End, although Devlyn had warned her that the view would be poor. It was difficult to see any of the giant rocks that were the feature of the place and the heavy mist billowed around them until Lenca felt cold and damp and dispirited. Sensing her mood, Devlyn drew her into the protection of his arm; under her new resolution Lenca did not resist. A gentle warmth stole through her and she smiled. The corners of his eyes crinkled in response and he pressed a brief kiss on her hair. So light that Lenca thought she had imagined it, but before she could dwell on the matter he said:

'I don't know about you, but I'm starving. Let's find somewhere to eat.'

'Oh, yes, please,' nodded Lenca. 'It must be the air down here. I've never eaten so well as I have these last few days.'

'Do you good,' he commented. 'You've already got some colour in your cheeks. You were a pale little thing when you arrived.'

'Thank you very much,' said Lenca in mock indignation, causing him to retort:

'Pale *and* interesting.'

'That's better,' she quipped. 'You made me sound like a waif and stray.'

'I didn't mean to. But you town people are all the same. We can pick you out easily.'

In comparison to his own swarthy complexion Lenca saw why. Here on the hillside, with the wind tangling his white curls and the brown column of his throat revealed by a partly open shirt, he looked very much the outdoor man. So virile, so strong; his masculinity overwhelmed her. She had not had many boyfriends – certainly none of Devlyn's type. It was difficult to imagine him in a nine-to-five office job. The sea was in his blood and that was where he belonged.

They had reached Penzance again before Devlyn stopped. He drove through the narrow streets, halting outside a low white brick building, which impressed her by its cleanliness and generally cheerful air.

'You'll like it here,' he said, and Lenca immediately saw why. It was fitted out with relics of old-time ships. They ate a superb meal downstairs in the 'Cabin' and then went upstairs to the 'Wreck Bar' for coffee. A model of a fully kitted skin diver stared down from his suspended position above their heads and close by stood another model – this time in an old-type diving suit complete with hard hat. A profusion of enormous plants, figureheads, and ship's bells were all around.

'Are all these genuine?' asked Lenca.

'I believe so,' he replied. 'Must have taken years to collect. Makes my own few souvenirs look sick.'

'Where do you keep your collection?' It was the first time Lenca had heard him mention his own discoveries and she was curious as to whether he had anything belonging to the *Valancia*.

'They're at my mother's house in Gloucester,' he said. 'One day I'll buy a house of my own – when I find someone to share it with – and then I can display my few humble treasures.'

He meant when he got married, thought Lenca, but why had he looked at her so oddly?

They left Penzance at about three. Devlyn selected a cassette and the haunting melody of Mendelssohn's *Spring Song* filled the car. Lenca settled back happily in her seat. She had enjoyed her meal and Devlyn's company and now looked forward to a pleasant ride home. He had revealed a different side to his nature today, going out of his way to be courteous, and she had surprised herself by responding. I shall have to be careful, she thought, with a wry pull of her lips, or I'll find myself falling for him. And why shouldn't you? called out an inner voice. You've seen what a delightful companion he can be. Agreed, she argued back, but I also know what he's after – a share in my grandfather's wealth.

'Penny for them.' Devlyn's voice interrupted her reasoning, a questioning twinkle in his eyes. But before she had time to answer the car gave a sudden splutter

54

and a jerk and rolled to a halt.

Uttering an oath beneath his breath, Devlyn pulled on the handbrake.

'What's happened?' enquired Lenca.

'Ask a stupid question,' he growled, opening his door and disappearing behind the bonnet.

Lenca remained in her seat, confident it was some minor fault and that he would soon get the car going again. A few minutes later, however, his head appeared round the door. 'Jump in the driver's seat,' he said, 'and try the engine when I tell you – and make sure it's out of gear.'

She slid obediently across and prepared to turn the key. He was so much taller that unless she sat on the edge of the seat her foot did not reach the accelerator, emphasizing the marked difference in their heights.

'Right – *now!*' he called, but nothing happened. Several times she tried until at last he slammed down the bonnet in exasperation. 'It's no good. She won't have it.' He wiped his greasy hands on a duster and leaned an elbow on the open door. His hair clung in tight, damp curls to his forehead and he had a black smudge across his nose. Lenca wanted desperately to laugh but knew she daren't. He was in no mood to appreciate her amusement.

'I don't know what's the matter,' he growled. 'She's never let me down before.' The sleek car had proved not as reliable as he thought, and Lenca sensed his chagrin.

'Never mind,' she said, in an attempt to soothe him. 'There's a garage down the road. Maybe they can help.'

'Let's hope so,' he sighed, and was away before Lenca could offer to accompany him.

He returned within minutes. 'They'll take a look if we get it there. Their pick-up's out on a job. It *would* be.' He sighed again. 'Steer it, will you, and I'll push. Lucky the road's flat. If this had happened on one of those hills heaven knows what we'd have done.'

Through the interior mirror Lenca saw Devlyn sweating and straining and for the first time felt sorry for him. Several cars passed, but not one offered assistance and Lenca could imagine his opinion of the British motorist at this particular point in time.

'Can't I help?' she yelled through the open window. 'The road's pretty straight here.'

'No, thanks. You stay there,' his voice breathless and uneven. 'Steer into the bay when we reach the garage.'

Half an hour later Devlyn acquainted Lenca with the news that no spare was available for the Alfa. The part had to be purchased from a specialist and could not be obtained before morning.

'What are we going to do?' Lenca looked at him in distress. 'It's half past four already. I'm supposed to be visiting Grandfather at six.'

'I'm afraid there's not much we can do,' admitted Devlyn, a frown creasing his brow. 'There's no bus that would take us all the way and they don't hire cars. I suggest you phone Daniel and then we find somewhere to stay for the night.'

Lenca's violet eyes fled open. 'B-but we can't! I mean—' A sudden suspicion entered her mind and she looked at him accusingly. 'You meant this to happen! You had it all planned. Well, if you think I'm going to spend the night with you – you're mistaken. I'll find my own way home – somehow.'

As she turned away Devlyn put a detaining hand on her shoulder. 'Be reasonable, Lenca. How could I plan a thing like this? If I'd known the car was going to break down I wouldn't have suggested a day out.'

'How do I know that?' stormed Lenca. 'You've probably arranged it with the mechanics here. What did you do? Slip them a fiver so they'd say they couldn't mend it until morning?'

She was furious. Did he think her gullible enough to believe his story? An expensive car like an Alfa didn't break down. He'd got to be joking if he thought she'd fall for that one. It was the age-old story all over again.

The only indication Devlyn gave that he was annoyed was the steeling of his eyes. His voice remained perfectly calm and even. 'Think what you like. The fact of the matter is that we're stuck here whether you like it or not. Now, are you going to ring Daniel or shall I?'

Although Lenca knew she judged Devlyn unfairly she was unable to accept the fact that this incident was not his fault. He should have checked the car before setting off, she grumbled to herself. What if they had been miles away from a garage? What would he have done then?

Devlyn had successfully booked them rooms at a nearby inn and ensured that everything was to her satisfaction, but even so Lenca was unable to respond to his efforts to make light of the situation. Throughout dinner she had maintained a stony silence and now as they sipped their coffee she stared broodingly down at her cup.

'I can't see what you hope to gain by this ridiculous attitude,' he said, eyeing her speculatively. 'I feel a right chump myself, offering to take you out for the day and this happening, without you making matters worse.'

Lenca raised her brows. 'You sound almost as though it was a genuine breakdown.'

'Good heavens, Lenca, it *was*! I'm not such a cad as to play a trick like that. Can't you forget it and enjoy the rest of the evening? Life's too short to be miserable.'

He gave an engaging grin, and Lenca could not help

57

but respond. She must have known all along that he wasn't fooling, yet some stubborn streak had made her resentful and say things she did not mean. 'I'm sorry, Devlyn, but it did look suspicious. I suppose I have been silly. Forgive me.'

He heaved a dramatic sigh. 'Thank goodness for that! I thought this feud would go on for ever. Who was it who said *Hell hath no fury like a woman scorned?*'

'I've no idea,' laughed Lenca, 'but I bet it was a man.'

'How would you like some brandy with your coffee?' he asked, and without waiting for her reply signalled the waiter to bring two glasses.

The rest of the evening passed in a haze. Devlyn made no secret of the fact that he found her attractive, and Lenca could not help but feel a heady response.

'You're very beautiful,' he murmured after they had found a quiet corner in the lounge. 'Those eyes – they bewitch me.'

'And you're a flatterer,' retorted Lenca.

'No – I mean it,' he said earnestly. 'You've inherited the Trevelyan good looks – not their build, though. You're so tiny and fragile that I feel I want to put you in a glass case to protect you.'

'I'm not as delicate as I look,' protested Lenca, nevertheless pleased by his compliments. What woman wouldn't delight in being treated as though she were a precious possession? She thought the whisky he had downed might have a lot to do with his mellow, expansive mood, but even so it was enjoyable basking in the warmth of his praise. She was prepared to forget for a while her misgivings and accept what the evening had to offer.

'That remains to be seen,' he smiled. 'Diving can be

58

an exhausting pastime, especially if you're not used to it.'

Perhaps he was hoping she might give up the idea, pondered Lenca, but she wouldn't spoil the evening by saying so. Instead she returned his smile. 'Will you take me tomorrow, if the weather's cleared?'

'I can't refuse when you look at me like that,' he replied. 'The pleading in your eyes is enough to melt a heart of stone. Kip noticed it too. I saw the way he looked at you over dinner last night.'

'Is that why you objected?' taunted Lenca. 'Were you jealous?'

His fair brows lifted imperceptibly and his blue eyes danced. 'Would you like me to be? Seriously, though, I really was concerned. He's a good diver but not experienced in these waters.'

Lenca's heart skipped unaccountably at the notion that Devlyn was jealous of Kip. A sudden warmth ran through her, but she rejected the idea that she was becoming fond of him. Good food and wine were the reasons for her change of heart. In the harsh light of morning she would see him in his true glory. Meanwhile it was pleasant to be pampered and made to feel the most important person in his life . . .

It was mid-afternoon before the car was ready and nearly five when they reached Trevelyan Manor. 'Afraid it's too late for diving now,' pronounced Devlyn as they slid to a halt. 'Pity, today would have been ideal. Let's hope tomorrow's the same.'

It had indeed been a glorious day. Lenca had woken with the sun streaming through her bedroom window and after breakfast Devlyn had suggested a walk, first checking at the garage how long it would be before the car was ready. They had crossed fields and meadows, wandered down isolated lanes, drunk cider outside a tiny inn. It had been one of the happiest days Lenca could remember. Devlyn had been fun. He had treated her as an equal, a friend – with an element of affection thrown in. Although she knew he was displeased by his car breaking down he was everything a woman could ask for – attentive, courteous, teasing. Not once did they have cross words, and when he caught her hand to help her over a stile Lenca experienced again the warm glow of the evening before. Only this time she couldn't blame it on the drink . . .

Meg was in the hall as they entered and her lined face broke into a smile. 'Thank goodness you're back! I was fair worried when you phoned last night. Is the car all right now, Master Devlyn?'

'Yes, thank you, Meggie,' placing his arm affectionately round the housekeeper's shoulders. 'Everything's just fine. How about something to eat, I'm starving.'

'That's nothing unusual,' she retorted. 'Tell me when you're not! I'll make some tea to tide you over – we'll have dinner early.'

'Not for me, Meg,' said Lenca, moving towards the staircase. 'I'm off to visit Grandfather. Keep mine warm, I'll have it later.'

'What's the rush?' Devlyn turned and regarded her closely. 'Another hour won't make much difference. You've got to eat.'

The concern on his face caused Lenca's heartbeats to quicken and she looked away. She had thought that once back at the Manor the rapport that had existed between them since last night would disappear, that she would once again see him as a gold-digger. But this was not so. His very nearness was turning her legs to jelly and she caught hold of the curved handrail for support.

'You don't know my car. It takes me nearly two hours.'

'Then I'll take you.' His smile was warm and all-embracing. 'It's time I visited Daniel.' He turned again to Meg, who had been watching this by-play with interest. 'That's settled. Dinner as soon as you can and a pot of tea to keep us going. I'll fetch it as soon as I've washed and changed.'

'Bless you!' beamed the housekeeper as she bustled away towards the region of the kitchen.

Lenca knew that Meg wondered what had gone on between Devlyn and herself, and hurried up the stairs so that he would not see her flaming face.

'Hey, wait for me!' he called, racing up behind and catching her a smart pat on the behind as he did so.

'Ouch!' yelled Lenca. 'What was that for?'

'For going without me,' he grinned. 'You seem mighty eager to be rid of me now. Had enough of my company?'

'It's not that.' Lenca avoided his eyes and continued to hurry along the corridor. 'I – I just want to get out of these clothes, that's all.'

'Little liar!' he whispered fiercely, pulling her round to face him.

Lenca thought for one moment that he was going to kiss her and struggled frantically to free herself. She was not ready for that – yet. She needed time to analyse her feelings. Everything had happened so quickly.

He released her immediately. 'You look like a startled fawn with those big soulful eyes. Did I frighten you? I'm sorry.' He reached out a hand and stroked her cheek. 'Why, you're trembling. What's the matter?'

She shook her head. 'Nothing. It's hurrying up those stairs.' But still she avoided his eyes.

61

'I don't believe you,' he said softly, 'but we'll leave it at that – for now. Have a hot bath. I'll bring your tea up if you like and you can rest till dinner.'

'Oh, no!' The thought of him in her bedroom caused even more consternation. 'I mean, it's all right, I'll come down. I'm not tired, honestly.'

One eyebrow quirked disbelievingly, but he nodded. 'Okay, you know best.'

He watched as she walked towards her room and Lenca felt relieved once the door had closed behind her. Alone at last she could examine her newly awakened senses.

Was this love she felt? In all her twenty years she had never experienced feelings like these – the sudden racing of her pulses when his cornflower blue eyes met hers, the weakening of her limbs at his touch. Many of her friends had proclaimed such sensations when falling in love. But surely love went deeper than that? Love meant wanting to belong; to share; to know that the rest of your life would be meaningless without him. Was this how she felt about Devlyn? She shook her head in confusion. After their stormy beginning she couldn't possibly love him. It was animal magnetism, that was all, she decided. It would be useless to deny his physical attraction. His seadog air and perfect physique were enough to excite any woman. She was allowing herself to get all worked up over nothing. He'd probably treated her no differently from anyone else, yet here she was acting like some lovesick schoolgirl after her first date. She must try to keep her emotions under stricter control. His all too blue eyes saw more than they should, and some things were best kept to herself.

Even so, on their journey to the hospital the fuchsia hedgerows had never seemed so pretty, the sky never before been so bright a blue or the clouds so delicate and lacy. Devlyn remained silent as though sensing her need for peace; the only sound was the hum of tyres against the grey ribbon of the road and the unsteady pulsing of Lenca's heart. She glanced surreptitiously across at her companion. He smiled softly without turning his head. 'Would you like some music?'

'Mmm, please,' nodded Lenca. He seemed attuned to her every need and she wriggled more comfortably in her seat, resting her head against the soft upholstery listening to the strains of the Pastoral Symphony. His taste in music amazed her. She thought he would have preferred something modern. Yet was she really surprised? The book of poetry should have told her that he was a man of depth, and now this – it was beautiful. She closed her eyes allowing the sounds to envelop her completely.

Devlyn's touch brought her to with a start. 'We're there. Are you ready?'

Guiltily Lenca looked up into his smiling eyes, realizing that she had fallen asleep. 'I'm sorry,' she said quickly, 'I didn't mean to—'

'Don't apologize,' he cut in. 'It's a compliment that you should find my company so relaxing – unless you were bored?'

'Not at all,' she assured him. 'I enjoyed the music.'

'I thought you would. We have kindred tastes, you and I.'

Lenca wondered how he could be sure when they hardly knew one another, but she smiled and uncurling as gracefully as a kitten allowed him to help her from the car, missing his look of admiration as she bent to straighten her skirt.

Daniel Trevelyan sat in the same place by the window, tapping his fingers impatiently on the arm of his chair. Lenca went in first, dropping her usual kiss on his cheek.

'There you are,' he began brusquely. 'What've you been up to? Thought you'd forgotten all about me.'

'I told you we'd broken down,' protested Lenca. 'We've only just got back.'

'Well, you'd better tell that young man to get himself a decent car before he takes my granddaughter out again. And where is he? Why hasn't he been to see me? Wait till I get out of here, I'll—'

'You'll what?' Devlyn's voice came deep and amused from behind the door. 'What are you up to, you old fraud? There's not much wrong, by the sound of it.'

Daniel beamed as his young friend came towards him. 'Devlyn, my boy, it's good to see you!'

'And it's good to see you, Daniel. What have you been doing to yourself? Never thought I'd find you in a place like this.'

'Didn't think so myself. But I'll be out soon, never fear. How's the dive going?'

'Er – slowly.' A second's hesitation before Devlyn answered; a second in which Lenca saw the quick glance he slanted at the older man. He's wondering whether Grandfather's suspicious, she thought. How could he not be when Devlyn came to this particular spot year after year? He must be aware that something attracted him here. Had they discussed the *Valancia*? It seemed natural to assume they had, yet her grandfather had swept aside her questions regarding this, giving the impression that it was none of Devlyn's business.

'Weather stopped play yesterday,' continued Devlyn.

'So you took Lenca out? Admirable, my boy. Thought you didn't get on? Leastways, that's what she said,' nodding his head towards his granddaughter.

'Well, we didn't,' retorted Lenca defensively. 'He was perfectly horrible towards me when we first met.'

'And now?' interposed Devlyn with a grin.

'You've changed,' reluctantly. 'You – you're quite – nice, now.' Lenca felt the colour steal into her cheeks, unaware of how attractive she looked, her eyes dark and faintly luminous like twin jewelled orbs in her elf-like face.

'He's quite nice! Is that all you can say?' snorted her grandfather. 'He's a damn fine fellow. You'll need go a long way to find another like him.'

Too true, thought Lenca. There could never be another Devlyn. He was in a class of his own. But whether her grandfather was aware of his avaricious streak she did not know – and she could not very well ask without rousing his wrath. He was obviously very fond of Devlyn and would hear no word against him.

'Has Lenca told you I'm going to teach her to dive?' asked Devlyn, with a swift change of subject. 'She's shown great interest in our activities. I think she wants to have a go for herself.'

Daniel looked at his granddaughter strangely before saying, 'Look after her well, Devlyn. She's all I've got.'

'Trust me,' said the younger man. 'I won't let her get into trouble.'

'Mmm,' nodded her grandfather, but he was un-usually quiet after that and when the two prepared to leave he called Lenca back.

'If you're thinking of trying to find Edward's treasure,' he whispered hoarsely, 'forget it. Think of your father – and my brother. Don't let the Manacles claim anyone else. You mean so very much to me.'

His eyes were ominously bright as he grasped Lenca's hand. All she could do was nod her head and swallow the sudden constricting lump in her throat.

CHAPTER FOUR

LENCA's heart beat rapidly as she went down to breakfast the next morning. It had every promise of being another fine, sunny day. Very soon she would be having her first lesson and she could not help but feel apprehensive.

The four men were already at the table, but it was towards Devlyn she looked first. Dressed in blue sweater and jeans he looked every inch a seafaring man, and her heart did a funny little flip as his eyes met hers. For just one second she forgot they were not alone; her lips smiled tremulously, her eyes shone; then awareness that they were being observed by three pairs of very interested eyes caused her to look away and greet the other members of the team.

'They're all dying to know what happened,' ventured Devlyn. 'I hadn't the nerve to tell them myself. I said they must ask you.'

He clearly felt deeply that his car had let him down, thought Lenca. Best to turn the whole affair into a joke. So in an exaggerated whisper she said, 'His car broke down. We spent the night in an inn.'

Alan looked from one to the other, a knowing smile on his face. 'Devlyn, you crafty old so-and-so! How did you get away with it?'

'Trust you to think the worst,' retorted Devlyn. 'It's true. My trustworthy steed failed me.'

'Lucky you,' quipped Kip, his eyes lingering on Lenca.

'What do you mean, lucky?' protested Devlyn. 'Lenca thought, like you, that I'd done it on purpose. I had the devil of a job persuading her it was genuine.'

'I bet you did,' laughed Trevor, and they all joined in. But Lenca knew their ribaldry was good-natured and took no offence.

'Looking forward to your lesson?' asked Kip as their meal drew to a close.

'Yes and no,' replied Lenca, glancing swiftly towards Devlyn to see if he was listening, but he was deep in conversation with Alan. 'I want to learn, but I feel a bit nervous. I don't know quite what to expect.'

'Don't worry. Devlyn's a marvellous teacher. He'll instil confidence without you realizing it.'

'I hope so. I don't want to do anything silly.'

'Of course you won't,' insisted Kip. 'Just do what he says and you'll find yourself diving without any effort at all. Once you start you'll never want to stop. It's like a drug. I live for my holidays when I can spend all my time in the sea.'

'It's not your living, then?'

'Oh, gosh, no. I couldn't make a living from it. It's a hobby, I suppose. I'm a draughtsman by trade.'

'I wouldn't have believed it,' laughed Lenca. 'You look as though you spend your life out of doors.'

'I do, as much as I can, believe me. But I enjoy my work and I've always got this to look forward to.'

Lenca looked up as Devlyn dropped a hand on her shoulder. 'We'd best get going if you want that lesson.'

'Of course.' She twisted free and faced him, slightly breathless. 'W-what do I wear?'

'Under your wet suit?' His lips curved wickedly, but his voice was all innocence. 'Nothing!' And when she looked at him outrageously he laughed. 'Wear a swim-suit, if you like, and don't forget a towel.'

He was in the hall when she came back downstairs, the others having already left. He pursed his lips in a soundless whistle. 'You should always wear green,' he said. 'It suits you. You look like a little pixie this morning – ready to bewitch me.'

She gave a wan smile. 'Please, don't tease. I'm scared enough as it is.'

'I'm not teasing – it's true.' His breath was close to her ear, one arm touching her shoulder.

The tingling awareness was there again and Lenca hurried towards the door. 'Let go,' she said, 'before I change my mind.'

'You can if you like,' answered Devlyn, suddenly serious. 'I wouldn't force you to do anything you didn't want to.'

'It's not that. I want to learn, really I do.' Even though I know you'd like nothing better than for me to back out now, she thought, suddenly remembering how he had tried to dissuade her. 'It's just nerves – like going to the dentist, or starting a new job. It will pass once we start.'

He opened the door and within seconds they were in the car, purring along the drive. Instead of turning left out of the gates towards Porthoustock as Lenca had anticipated, they went in the opposite direction.

'We'll go to Porthkerris,' said Devlyn in answer to her questioning look. 'It's much quieter there. You don't want a crowd of spectators on your first lesson.'

Lenca was both surprised and pleased by this show of consideration. He was the most amazing man she had ever met – in more ways than one.

Porthkerris turned out to be far prettier than Porthoustock. It was reached by a steep, narrow hill, that caused Lenca to cling apprehensively to her seat, but it was well worth the journey, she decided, when they at last reached the bottom.

High cliffs towered on either side, rocks jutted out

into the sea forming sheltered pools near the shore, seagulls wheeled overhead. It was altogether a perfect setting and just as Lenca had imagined Cornwall should be. She turned to Devlyn excitedly. 'Isn't it beautiful? I'm so glad you've brought me here.'

'I knew you'd like it,' he smiled. 'There'll probably be a few more people down later – mainly divers. But for the time being we'll have the place to ourselves.'

He opened the boot of his car and Lenca saw the black rubber suits and fins, the air bottles and face masks, and felt a surge of excitement. Only one thing seemed strange. 'Where's the boat?' she asked.

'Don't rush things,' he laughed. 'There's a lot to learn before you think of diving in deeper waters.'

'I see.' Somehow she had visualized jumping straight over the side. She had not realized she had to learn in stages.

He reached out two suits. 'This one should fit. It was the smallest I could find. Now watch me and do the same.'

Without a trace of self-consciousness he stripped off his sweater and trousers, folding them neatly and placing them in the boot. His brief black swimming trunks revealed the muscular power of his tanned body, and Lenca felt a sudden urge to run her hands over the smooth brown skin.

Repressing the thought immediately, she unfastened her dress. Realizing how delicate and pale she was in comparison and afraid he might scoff, she turned her back as she slipped the green cotton from her shoulders, exposing the paler shade of her swimsuit.

He watched as she put her clothes beside his, but far from deriding her he pulled her into his arms and rained kisses on her sleek brown hair. For a second Lenca allowed herself to respond before raising startled eyes to his. Immediately he released her. 'I'm sorry, but you're so enchanting I can't resist you. And if I'm right — you like me a little bit too?'

It was more than a little, she told herself, but she had no intention of revealing to Devlyn yet exactly how much he was beginning to mean to her. 'A teeny bit,' she teased, 'but I thought you'd brought me here to dive, not flatter me with your attentions.'

'So I have,' he said in mock solemnity. 'Let's get kitted up.'

She watched as he pulled on his skin-tight rubber diving suit and copied his actions to get into her own outfit. It felt strange and stiff at first, but after a few moments she became accustomed to the feel of it against her skin.

'We'll try snorkelling first,' he said, 'to get you used to looking under water. It's surprising how different everything appears.'

He showed her how to adjust the face mask so that it fitted properly, then with the snorkel in position they waded out until they reached a depth suitable for swimming. The water felt cold as it crept inside her suit, but within seconds it reached body temperature and Lenca felt wonderfully warm.

'Put the mouthpiece in now,' instructed Devlyn, 'then bend forward and place your face in the water and practise breathing through your mouth. Some people forget and try to breathe through their nose.'

After a few seconds Lenca found she could breathe quite easily.

'Good, very good. Now we'll try swimming. If you get any water into your tube, don't panic. Resurface, then blow hard through your mouth. The tube will clear and you'll be able to start again.'

After a few minutes practising like this they returned

to the shore.

'What do you think?' asked Devlyn.

'It was marvellous. I could see fish and all sorts of things I never knew existed.'

'You've seen nothing yet,' he laughed. 'Wait until you get into really deep water. But next we'll put on the fins to give you more mobility.'

Lenca was surprised at the patience Devlyn showed in teaching her these basic principles of skin diving. It must have been boring for him, she thought afterwards, but at no time did he show the slightest sign of tediousness, and she herself felt thrilled by the whole new world it opened up.

'We'll try it with the aqualung next,' he said, as they sat on the beach recovering from Lenca's latest efforts and drinking coffee from the flask he had so thoughtfully provided. 'Are you sure you want to carry on? It's not too much?'

Lenca shook her head vigorously, while swallowing her scalding coffee. 'I told you I was stronger than I look. I can't wait to get down to the real nitty-gritty.'

'You're a devil for punishment,' he laughed, lying back on the blanket with his hands behind his head. 'You'll probably ache all over in the morning. Don't say I haven't warned you.'

'Very well, master.' Lenca gave him a mock salute and lay back beside him. The sun was warm against her face, but it was not the sun that caused this glow that enveloped her body. It was this blond giant of a man at her side. She turned her head slowly and studied his profile. His eyes were closed and his lashes, which were ridiculously long for a man, she decided indignantly, fanned his cheeks. His nose was slightly crooked, as though it had been broken at some time in his life, and a fine scar disappeared into his hairline above his left ear. She hadn't noticed it before and wondered what had caused it.

As though aware of her scrutiny Devlyn rolled his head to one side and opened his eyes. 'What's your verdict? Do I pass?'

'I'm sorry, I didn't mean to be rude.'

'I know. You're just curious as to what makes a man like me attracted towards a girl like you.' He looked again at the sky and seemed to be talking more to himself than to Lenca. 'I always thought that when I fell in love it would be after a long friendship with someone of my own type – one of the girls from the diving club, maybe. Yet here I am, completely head over heels almost without knowing it had happened. You bewitched me from the first moment I saw you – you know that? You've crept under my skin, and I'm going to made darn sure than you don't escape.'

Lenca had gone first hot and then cold at this revelation, and now she sprang to her feet and walked a few steps away. Devlyn loved her! He loved her! *And she loved him!* Yes, she did – despite everything. So why this sense of foreboding? Why didn't she fling herself into his arms and admit that she felt the same? What stopped her?

Some sixth sense warned her that things were moving too quickly. She had never before been in love and must make sure before committing herself. Why, oh, why had Devlyn mentioned it this morning? Why hadn't he waited until their friendship had progressed a little further? Only two days ago they had argued bitterly, and now he professed to love her.

Suddenly she felt his touch on her arm. Regardless of the fact that they were both clad in rubber diving suits he swung her round and pulled her close, tilting her chin so that she was forced to look into his eyes. 'Have I distressed you? I thought that – no, I was sure you felt the same way about me. Maybe I shouldn't have sprung it on you like this. Perhaps you'd prefer candle-light and music?'

Lenca smiled weakly. 'It is a bit sudden. I need time to think about it.'

He frowned. 'Think about what? Whether you love me? That shouldn't give you any cause for thought. Or whether you want to marry me? Is that what you want time for?'

'M-marry you?' Events were moving too quickly for Lenca. 'You didn't say anything about wanting to marry me.'

'Do I have to? Maybe I'm old-fashioned, but I thought love and marriage went together.'

'So they do, b-but—'

'I'm rushing you, is that it?'

Lenca nodded. She couldn't have spoken if she had wanted. At that particular moment words failed her.

His kiss was long and infinitely tender. She could feel his heart beating through the thin rubber of their suits and her own answering response that she was unable to control. She felt dizzy with emotion and had he released her would have fallen to the ground.

He traced the soft outline of her cheek with a gentle forefinger and his eyes were a deeper blue than ever before. 'Tell me tomorrow,' he whispered, pulling her back down on to the blanket. 'Rest a while now and then we'll carry on with the lesson.'

'I – I don't think I want to.' The thought of spending more time in his company was unbearable. She needed to be alone. It was impossible to think coherently with him so near; he hazed her thoughts.

'You're not giving up after all the fuss you made?' But he was smiling and Lenca knew he only teased.

73

'Of course not. Is there any coffee left? Perhaps that will help. I feel very weak all of a sudden.'

'Sounds promising,' he grinned, 'if I have that effect on you.'

'How do you know it's you?' scoffed Lenca. 'It could be the swimming.'

'Don't disappoint me. You'll deflate my ego,' handing her a brimming cup.

'Impossible. You're the most conceited man I've ever come across. I remember thinking that the first time we met — when you sat in my grandfather's armchair acting as though you owned the place. I hated you.'

He grinned. 'That's interesting. I don't need to tell you the old saying that hate's akin to love?'

Lenca aimed a blow at his leg, but he dodged neatly and sprang to his feet. 'Let's carry on, or it will be lunch time before we know where we are.'

Once in the water Devlyn became again the expert teacher and Lenca was able to forget for a while that he had suddenly and surprisingly proposed to her.

With the aqualung now strapped to her back and a weight belt round her waist, he led her to a position several yards from the shore and told her to sit on the bottom to get used to breathing under water. 'This is when you find out whether you'll make a diver,' he said. 'Some people suffer from claustrophobia and can never master the technique. Remember, breathe normally.'

At first Lenca forgot his instructions and took in great gulps of air, but before long she became used to the idea that she could breathe perfectly naturally with air from the tank and became impatient sitting on the bottom doing nothing.

She tapped his leg and he reached down to help her

up. 'You're doing marvellously,' he said. 'Much better than I expected. I must admit I had my doubts, but you're not bad, for a little one.'

He made sure she knew how to clear her mask should it flood with water, and various other safety procedures before suggesting they fin their way round the surrounding headland.

To Lenca it was an experience never to be forgotten – her first underwater trip. It was like being in an entirely different world. A change of element – a change of time. Thick weeds grew like a dense pine forest, fish of all shapes and sizes swam past without a glance at the alien creatures invading their territory. It was all so wonderful. Lenca felt exhilarated.

Finning at her side, Devlyn looped his thumb and forefinger together – the diver's okay signal. Lenca answered in the same manner. She felt she could go on all day and was unreasonably sad when he eventually guided her back.

Once on dry land she found out how much energy she had really used. Her legs felt like jelly and she was glad of Devlyn's helping hand as they made their way back to the car. He took off her air bottle, and flinging her fins and face mask to one side she threw herself down on the blanket, regardless of the fact that her suit was dripping.

Devlyn stood over her, laughing. 'Had enough?'

'Yes, thanks. But it was wonderful. I wouldn't have missed it for the world. Can we come again tomorrow?'

'Hold on. I've got my work to do. But we'll see – as you're such a good pupil.'

He had his own gear off now and clad only in trunks flung himself down beside her. 'Take your suit off. It will dry in the sun.'

Lenca obeyed, but felt suddenly too shy to lie back

beside him. Instead she walked over to where the rocks tumbled into the sea and began exploring the pools left by the tide. She needed to get away for a space to sort out her confusion of thoughts and to find out why she was hesitant about giving him a definite answer. She loved him – or thought she did – and he professed to love her, so what was the problem? She viewed the situation from every conceivable angle, but was still unable to resolve it. Perhaps she didn't really love him, she concluded. That seemed the only solution, even though every fibre of her being told her otherwise. He only had to touch her to set her pulses on fire.

Finding a flat, smooth rock, she sat down and drew her knees into the circle of her arms, looking out over the silvery surface of the sea. Gently it lapped at the boulders beneath her feet. Closing her eyes, she lost herself for a few seconds in the serenity of her surroundings. Never before had she found such peace. Today would have been perfect had Devlyn not spoilt everything by proposing. She wasn't ready for marriage yet – not to him or anyone. She needed time to get used to her new way of life; time to enjoy the freedom she had never known when her mother was alive. Much as Lenca had loved her mother, Miriam Trevelyan had been a very possessive woman and Lenca had had little time she could call her own.

So immersed in thought was she that she did not hear Devlyn's soft footsteps as he crossed the rocks towards her. She was not aware of his presence until he put a hand about her shoulder and sat on the rock beside her. He had changed into jeans and sweater, and silently they watched a ship moving across the horizon. He did not speak. It was as though he appreciated her desire for quietude. Gently he pulled her head down on to his shoulder and together they remained for a minute – an hour? Lenca knew not how long. Time stood still as she allowed this huge and strangely gentle man to hold her in his arms. It was as though they were the last two people left on earth, and Lenca was reluctant to move for fear of breaking the spell.

Then suddenly their silence was rudely disturbed.

'Hi there!'

It was Alan, with Kip and Trevor following in his wake. Lenca turned her head and watched their progress over the rocks. Devlyn mumbled something, but made no attempt to release her.

'Thought we'd find you here,' said Alan, grinning mischievously. 'What's happened to the diving lesson, or has Lenca changed her mind?'

Devlyn's arm tightened about her shoulders as he spoke. 'Lenca's proved a very apt and promising pupil and is now enjoying a well-deserved rest. Where's your tact, man? Couldn't you see we didn't want to be disturbed?'

'Sorry, sir,' said Alan, still grinning. 'But we thought you might like to see this,' opening his hand to reveal a man's gold ring in the shape of a coiled serpent. It was worn as though by much wear and Lenca observed that there had once been a stone of some sort set in the eye.

'Let me see.' Devlyn rose quickly and almost snatched up the ring in his haste. 'Where did you find it?'

'Near where you were diving on Monday.'

Devlyn's eyes narrowed. 'You shouldn't have been there, but never mind now. You did right in bringing it to me.' He slipped the ring into his pocket, and although Lenca would have liked a closer look she felt that this was not the time to ask. She had the uncanny feeling that he did not want her to see the ring, and it was not difficult to guess why.

'I suggest we all go back to the Manor for lunch.' There was a strange urgency in Devlyn's voice that had not been there before. 'I'm sure Meg won't mind rustling up a few sandwiches – what do you think, Lenca?'

'I'll do them myself if Meg's busy,' her own tones dull and flat in contrast.

Devlyn surged ahead as they returned to the cars and it was Kip who gave Lenca a helping hand over the more difficult boulders.

Lenca slipped her dress over her already dry swimsuit as Devlyn started the engine. He scarcely spoke on the journey home. She tried asking about the ring, but he appeared reluctant to discuss it and in the end she gave up and gazed out of the window.

It was not difficult to see how his mind worked. He was at last on the track of her ancestor's treasure and couldn't wait to recommence diving to see what else could be found. It looked as though this would be the end of her lessons. He wouldn't want to give up valuable time now when he had other more important things to claim his attention.

Strangely enough after lunch he made no attempt to accompany his friends back down to Porthoustock. Instead he announced his intention of going to visit her grandfather. 'You must be exhausted,' he said, 'after this morning, so I suggest you take a rest. I'll go to the hospital instead.'

'But I want to see Grandfather,' Lenca protested. 'He'll be expecting me. I'm not tired, really.'

He held up a hand. 'No, I insist. I'll give him your apologies and say you'll be along tomorrow. No arguments, now.'

He was out of the house before Lenca could say another word. She heard the car spring into life, tyres squealing as he turned round, then with a roar he disappeared down the drive.

He's in a remarkable hurry, mused Lenca. I wonder if he wants to show Grandfather the ring and find out for sure whether it was Edward Trevelyan's. 'I do hope not,' she said aloud. 'Otherwise Grandfather's going to be so disappointed when he can't claim it. And Devlyn too will be in for a surprise if he finds out about the will. I can't see him risking his life for a mere ten per cent. I'd love to see his face when he finds out!'

Sudden remembrance of a set of photographs in her grandfather's book depicting the lost jewellery made Lenca move into the library. She found the book and took it to the table. But there was no ring on those pages that looked anything like a gold serpent, nor when she scanned the print could she find any reference to such a ring.

There had been many wrecks on the Manacles, both known and unknown, so the chances of anyone finding anything belonging to one particular ship were slight. Yet both she and Devlyn, if her assumption was correct, had jumped to the conclusion that it belonged to the wreck of the *Valancia*. It was natural, she supposed, but in a way she hoped they were wrong. She didn't want to think of Devlyn as an opportunist.

Admittedly she had thought this in the beginning, but that was before she had got to know him properly. Now she was prepared to concede that she had been wrong. During the many hours spent together he had given her no reason at all to believe he was a gold-digger. Indeed he had not mentioned the *Valancia*, and if this was one of the things closest to his heart surely he would have been unable to refrain from mentioning it? She smiled softly to herself as she crossed the thick green carpet and slipped the book back on to the shelf.

Soon she realized that something was stopping it resuming its former position in line with the rest of the volumes. She groped in the space and pulled out several sheets of crumpled paper. Once removed the book slid easily into position.

About to throw the pages into the waste bin, Lenca paused. Best to check that they were of no importance. What she saw made her feel for the nearest chair before her legs gave way. Had her grandfather forgotten about this copy of the will? What was it doing here? And more important still, had Devlyn seen it?

It was impossible to expect that he hadn't. Perhaps it had originally been tucked between the pages of the book and later slipped out on to the shelf. Anyone reading the book would have seen it. All colour drained from Lenca's cheeks as she realized the full significance of what this meant.

Devlyn had read the will.

He *knew* that as an outsider he could only expect a meagre ten per cent of anything he found. But – as a member of the family – he could claim everything!

And what could be better than marrying Daniel Trevelyan's sole remaining heir?

CHAPTER FIVE

LENCA'S knuckles gleamed white as she gripped the arm of her chair. How gullible she had been! How naïve!

She lifted her hands to her cheeks, feeling them hot now against the cool of her fingers. The will had fluttered from her nerveless grasp; she picked it up and screwed it into a tight ball, holding it close in the palm of her hand.

Rising, she paced up and down. No wonder Devlyn was excited. His dream was close to becoming reality — or so he thought. Thank goodness she had found out in time. Another few days and it might have been too late.

She closed her eyes. It didn't bear thinking about. Strange how she had held back from saying yes, almost as though she had known something was going to happen. And now? What did she do now? Even as she pondered a slow, burning anger against Devlyn Quinn began to fill every corner of her body. How dared he plot against the Trevelyan family? How dared he try and worm his way into her own and her grandfather's heart with his devious ways? Daniel had fallen for him hook, line and sinker — it was easy to see that. It was up to her to try and make him see what sort of a person his young friend really was. Thoughtfully she smoothed out the pieces of paper and put them into her handbag. There might come a time when she needed them — as evidence.

Determined now to have nothing more to do with Devlyn Quinn during the remainder of his stay, she let herself out of the library, closing the door gently behind her. She did not feel like shutting it quietly. She felt like banging every door in the house. And because she felt like this she decided to go for a walk. The fresh air would soothe her ruffled nerves and calm her disquieted thoughts.

Without realizing where she walked Lenca found herself eventually on Porthoustock beach. Kip and his friends were hauling their boat up on to the beach. 'You look all in,' said Kip. 'I thought you were supposed to be resting.'

Lenca raised her brows. 'No need to tell me who said that. When I need His Highness to tell me what to do I'll ask him, until then he can mind his own business.'

'Crikey, what's happened?' Kip's mouth fell open in astonishment. 'I've never heard you talk like that before.'

'I've never been treated like this before,' she gritted. 'But I'm sorry, it has nothing to do with you. I've had a shock, that's all. I thought a blow of sea air might do me good.'

He looked at her wisely for a moment. 'Hang on, I know just the place.'

Within seconds he had taken off his diving gear, towelled himself dry and slipped into shirt and trousers. 'This way,' guiding her by the elbow. 'It's pretty steep, but there's a super view and we won't be disturbed.'

The side of the cliff had been cut away by old quarry workings, but Lenca managed the climb easily with the aid of Kip's ready hand and once on top with the fresh breeze blowing into her face she soon began to feel better. They walked in silence for a time before Kip pulled her down on to the grass. 'Like to tell me what's troubling you?'

Lenca sighed. 'I don't think I can. It's private.' She nibbled a blade of grass meditatively. 'What I will say is that I've found out something about Devlyn Quinn that's put me off him for life. I can't go further without telling you the whole story.' Her voice rose and she felt dangerously near to tears. 'He's a cheat and a swindler, and I hate him!'

Kip looked at her in alarm. 'Those are strong words. Are you sure they're justified? We all like Devlyn. I'm sure he wouldn't—'

'There are two sides to Mr. Quinn,' interrupted Lenca hastily. 'The side we all see – and the one he keeps to himself. And I've found out about the hidden side of his character.'

Kip shook his head. 'I wish I could believe you, Lenca. But, honestly, I've never known Devlyn anything but honest and truthful.'

'Let me put it this way,' said Lenca. 'He's trying to cheat my grandfather, and consequently me. And I'm going to make darn sure he doesn't. This is strictly between you and me, understand? I don't want it getting round to the other fellows. Even Grandfather doesn't know yet.'

Kip's eyes narrowed. 'You've quarrelled with Devlyn?'

'Not yet,' grimly. 'He's visiting Grandfather.'

'It's all double dutch to me,' said Kip, shaking his head, 'but if you don't want to tell me there's not much I can do. Remember, though, I'm always ready if you need a shoulder to cry on. How did the diving go this morning? Did you enjoy it?'

Grateful that he had changed the subject, Lenca nodded. 'It was lovely. I loved every minute. Trouble is, I don't want him to take me out again now,' and then, eagerly, 'Will you take me, Kip – tomorrow? I'm going to the hospital in the morning, but after lunch, perhaps?'

Kip frowned. 'There's nothing I'd like better. But you know what Devlyn said.'

'To hell with Devlyn! If you don't take me I shall go on my own.'

He smiled ruefully. 'You don't leave me much alternative. I hope you know what you're doing.'

'I do. I feel better already.' Just talking to Kip had helped and now she jumped lightly to her feet. 'Come on, let's get back to the house.'

Devlyn had still not returned when they sat down to dinner, and Kip tactfully kept the conversation going so that the other two did not realize Lenca was any different from her usual cheerful self. Nevertheless as soon as the meal was over Lenca went straight to her room. Her next meeting with Devlyn would be tricky and she wished to put off the evil moment for as long as possible.

Although Lenca had expected to lie awake far into the night sleep came almost as soon as her head touched the pillow. She dreamt that she and Devlyn were in an underwater world of their own. They were able to breathe without compressed air and swam about as easily and nimbly as the fishes with whom they nudged shoulders. On the seabed he served her a meal of lobster and oysters and afterwards held her hand, guiding her up towards the surface. She panicked for fear they would be unable to breathe once they reached the air of the world above. This was their world, here, under the sea. They would need special equipment to help them breathe up there.

As they broke surface she woke. Gasping and per-spiring, Lenca took a few seconds to realize that she had been dreaming — and after that it was difficult to sleep again. What time was it? she wondered, afraid to put on her light in case someone saw it and came to see what was wrong.

Many hours later the grey fingers of dawn streaked the sky and with the rising of the sun she slept. Meg's tap on the door announcing breakfast rudely awoke her.

Lenca smiled ruefully. 'I'm sorry, Meg, I have a headache. I think I'll stay here a little longer.' She hadn't really a headache. It was an excuse not to go downstairs until Devlyn was out of the house. She never wanted to see him again. The hurt that filled her body deepened as she recalled he was also deceiving her grandfather. Daniel was old, with maybe only a few more years to live. How could Devlyn do this to him?

'Shall I bring you an aspirin?' Meg was fond of Lenca and didn't like to see her so pale and drawn.

'No, thanks, Meg. I had a bad night, that's all. I'll go back to sleep.'

The housekeeper shook her head doubtfully, and moved towards the door. 'I'll be up later to see how you are. I can't stay – the men are wanting their breakfast.'

An hour or so passed before Lenca heard the door open again and soft footsteps cross the carpet. She opened her eyes, expecting to see Meg, but instead saw Devlyn observing her closely. 'Meg tells me you have a headache.'

'That's right,' she retorted coldly, 'and I'd like to be alone, if you don't mind.' Deliberately she closed her eyes and turned her head away. But instead of leaving as she had hoped he walked round the bed and faced her again.

Ironically he looked concerned 'Are you sure you didn't overdo the diving? I let you do rather more than I intended.'

'I have a headache, that's all,' insisted Lenca, wishing he would go away. She had made her mind up overnight not to argue, merely to treat him with cool indifference. Let him wonder what was the matter, she didn't care. It would suit her best if she never saw him again, but they would inevitably meet, so she intended making it clear that there would be no more cosy tête-à-têtes. Their relationship would be on a strictly impersonal basis from now on.

'Lenca.' He spoke softly. 'What's the matter? You're acting as though you don't want me here.'

'That's right,' she said abruptly.

'B-but why? Yesterday we were so friendly, and now—'

At last she opened her eyes. He was looking down, a puzzled frown creasing his brow. 'I don't understand you, Lenca — just tell me what I'm supposed to have done to make you — feel like this.'

'How do you know how I feel?' Lenca pulled the sheets up tightly round her neck. It was difficult to maintain her dignity lying in bed. This wasn't the way she had planned their first meeting. In her thoughts she had put herself at the advantage. Now it was he who had the advantage over her.

'It's easy to see,' he insisted. 'Very anti-Devlyn Quinn. And it's not your headache that's doing it either. So come on, out with it. What have I done?'

Lenca arched her delicate brows, her violet eyes wide and innocent. 'If you don't know, I'm sure I'm not going to tell you.'

He frowned at the honey-sweetness of her tone and before Lenca realized what he was doing had whipped the clothes from her bed and yanked her up so that she stood beside him. 'No one speaks to me like that and gets away with it.'

'How dare you!' she blazed. 'How dare you! Get out of here!'

'Not until you've answered my question.' His grip on her wrist tightened.

'Then let's say I've changed my mind,' said Lenca icily. 'I've had time to give the whole matter a good deal of thought and I've decided I don't want to marry you.'

'Fair enough,' he replied. 'I admit I sprang it on you rather suddenly. Maybe I ought to have waited. But that's no reason to treat me like an outcast. Surely we can still be friends?' He released her abruptly and picked up her housecoat. 'Here, put this on. You're shivering.'

Lenca was, but through temper, not cold. She shrugged into the coat and faced him. 'I don't even want your friendship.'

His eyes narrowed. 'But you're not prepared to tell me why?'

'That's right,' her chin jutting determinedly forward. He'd deny it anyway, so what was the use?

'And nothing I can say or do will make you change your mind?'

Lenca shook her head and turned away, suddenly sickened by the whole affair. He had actually looked hurt – when all the time the only reason he wanted to marry her was to ensure a share of her grandfather's fortune. 'Please go,' she said softly.

For one moment she thought he would refuse, then his footsteps sounded heavy across the carpet. The door opened and closed and when she looked round he had gone. For one long minute Lenca stared at the door. His reaction had not been quite what she had expected. He had appeared distressed, almost as though he really cared – which was nonsense, of course. He was only interested in her inheritance. She had turned up at Trevelyan Manor like an answer to his prayers. Instead of having to ingratiate himself further into her grandfather's good books he had seen marriage to herself as the perfect solution. And she had nearly allowed herself to fall victim of his charms. How stupid she had been! Her first instincts had been right. She recalled vividly the day they met, how she had mistrusted him even then. Why, oh, why had she not followed this intuition?

The roar of Devlyn's car a few minutes later told her that he had left the house. Quickly now she washed and dressed and went in search of Meg. She found her in the kitchen.

'So you're up at last.' The housekeeper looked at her keenly. 'You still look very pale. Are you sure you're all right?'

'Much better,' answered Lenca. 'I'll make myself a cup of tea and a slice of toast, if you don't mind, then I'm off to see Grandfather.'

'He'll be pleased to see you, I'm sure. Tell him everything's ready and waiting for when he comes home.'

'I will, don't worry. I know how tiresome he finds it in hospital. He's missed you, that's the trouble. The nurses haven't time for his cantankerous ways.'

Daniel looked very fit and happy when Lenca entered his room and gave her an unusually long kiss. 'Have you recovered? Devlyn told me how tired you were yesterday after your first diving lesson.'

Lenca pulled her chair up close beside him. 'I wasn't really tired, Grandfather. It was Devlyn's idea that I should rest.'

'Very right, too. How did the lesson go?'

'I loved every minute,' Lenca smiled. 'I never realized how fascinating it is under water. It's like being

88

in another world.'

'I know what you mean, lass,' nodding wisely. 'But don't get too fond of it. It's a cruel world as well as an interesting one.'

'Don't worry, I'll be careful.' She took his hand and stroked it affectionately. 'How are you today? You look very pleased with yourself. Have you good news?'

'If you mean am I coming out, I don't know. The nurses say soon, but they won't give me a definite date. No, it's your news I'm waiting for – well, come on. Are you or aren't you?'

Lenca shook her head, bewildered. 'Am I what, Grandfather? What are you talking about?'

He sighed impatiently. 'Devlyn's proposal, what else? He told me yesterday that he'd asked you – best piece of news I've heard since I've been in this place. You've accepted, of course?' The old grey eyes stared keenly at her, a new light in their depths that Lenca was afraid to dispel.

She averted her eyes. Why had Devlyn told Daniel? Surely this should have been kept private until she had given him her answer. Obviously the old man had anticipated her assent and would be very distressed when she told him the truth. But what else could she say? There was no point in beating about the bush. Her grandfather would have to know sooner or later.

'I'm sorry to disappoint you,' she said evenly. 'I've turned him down.'

The light faded and he looked suddenly very old and very tired. 'Why, girl, why?' he whispered. 'He's a fine man – you'll find none better.'

Lenca clung to his hand imploringly. 'I don't love him, Grandfather.' She must make him believe that this was the truth. Seeing his face now she could not tell him about Devlyn. It would be too much for him to bear if he found out that Devlyn was nothing but a mercenary treasure-hunter. On the other hand he had become so attached to the younger man that he probably wouldn't believe her if she did try to explain.

'Pah! What's love?' he exploded. 'Plenty of people marry without love and are perfectly happy. You could learn to love him. Maybe he rubbed you up the wrong way to start with, but he's a nice boy deep down. Think about it, Lenca. Tell him you want a while longer to make up your mind.'

'It's no use. I *have* made up my mind, and nothing will change it.' She hated hurting her grandfather like this. Oh, what a fool Devlyn was to have told him. Did he think it would help matters if he had Daniel on his side? 'Don't upset yourself.' She laid her hand against his cheek and was startled to feel how cold he was.

He caught her hand roughly and pressed it to his lips. 'I'm a selfish old man. Don't listen to me. Of course your happiness comes first. It's just that – I had hoped—' He shrugged and released her, his eyes now fixed on the distant hills. It was almost as though he had forgotten his visitor, and when she looked at him she was appalled at the change these last few minutes had wrought to his lined old face. He looked ill again, as he had the day he came into hospital. And it's all my fault, she thought. I've done this to him.

He had set his heart on her marrying Devlyn and now she had disappointed him. But what else could she do? It would have been an even worse shock for him to find out that Devlyn was only after his money. He'll come to terms with it in time, she decided, trying to console herself for her guilty conscience. But on one account she was determined. She would have a jolly good try to find Edward Trevelyan's treasure herself. It was the only thing guaranteed to make her grandfather happy, and then perhaps he would forgive her for not agreeing to marry Devlyn.

Daniel remained staring out of the window in a broody silence. All Lenca's attempts to draw him into conversation failed, and she decided to leave, biting her lip vexedly when he ignored her farewells. He was being unnecessarily cruel, hurting her as much as she had hurt him. She hoped that tomorrow he would feel differently, and pressing her lips lightly to his cheek she left.

Her heels made little noise on the rubber-covered floor of the corridor and her thoughts were back there with the old man she had so needlessly offended. She could understand his reaction. As if he hadn't enough to contend with over the undiscovered treasure chests she had added to his burden. If only there were some way she could enlighten him as to his so-called friend — without causing too much anguish. But how? No matter which way she looked at her problem she was no nearer a solution.

Back at Trevelyan Manor Lenca ate a solitary lunch. There was no sign of Kip. It looked as though everything was fated to go wrong today. She had even forgotten to ask her grandfather about the serpent ring, although if it had been of any importance he would surely have mentioned it.

Just then Kip burst into the room. 'Sorry I couldn't make it any earlier. We had such a good dive this morning Devlyn kept us at it.'

'Does he know you're here now?' He wouldn't be very pleased if he knew what was happening.

Kip nodded. 'I had to tell him. He'd have probably seen us anyway and then there would have been more trouble. I don't suppose you've solved your dispute?' he finished hopefully.

Lenca shook her head. 'That's one thing you can be sure will never happen. Devlyn and I are finished.'

'I'm sorry,' and then he laughed. 'But what am I saying? Why should *I* be sorry? Perhaps there'll be a chance for me now. You're very attractive, and—'

'Please,' Lenca caught his arm, her eyes pleading. 'I like you a lot, Kip, but let's leave it at that. I'm not ready for anything else.'

'Okay,' he agreed. 'So long as I know there's a chance. You don't absolutely hate and detest me, do you?'

Lenca had to laugh at his comic expression. 'Of course not. You know very well what I mean. Are you ready to go? Have you had lunch?'

'I'm not hungry,' he replied, 'but as you've just eaten I think we ought to wait a while before you go in the water.'

'Okay. How about a walk in the grounds? I don't suppose you've had time to see much of the gardens – neither have I, come to think of it.'

'Suits me. Show the way and I'll follow.'

The garden, which was so big as to be almost a park, sprawled charmingly around the house. There were no formal flower beds, no regimental paths, and Lenca enjoyed the feeling of freedom it gave as they wandered slowly across grassy slopes and through sparse woodland. They followed the sound of running water and discovered a meandering stream shimmering in the bright sunlight. Lenca knelt down and let the water trickle through her fingers. It was clear and cold and when she raised her hand to her lips it tasted sweet and fresh.

'Do you live in the country?' she asked, as he squatted down beside her. 'Or are you a town bird like me?'

'I enjoy the best of both worlds,' he grinned. 'I live

near Epping Forest, but I work in London. I wouldn't have it any other way.'

'What made you interested in diving?'

'A friend of mine showed me some gold coins he'd discovered, and from then on I was hooked. I spend every available holiday diving.'

'Have you found anything interesting this time?' Lenca picked up a handful of pebbles and skimmed them one by one across the stream.

'I'll say,' said Kip enthusiastically. 'Only this morning I found what Devlyn is sure is part of the *Leeuw*'s bell.'

'How about the ring Alan found yesterday? Do you think that's from the *Leeuw* as well?'

Kip did not realize that Lenca was baiting him, that in fact she was trying to ascertain whether they had found anything belonging to the *Valancia* – without actually putting it into so many words. He frowned. 'I don't think so. As far as I know the *Leeuw* wasn't carrying treasure of any kind. And Alan *had* wandered away from the area we're searching. It's my guess that there's more where that came from – only Devlyn won't let us look. One job at a time is his maxim.'

'That's hardly fair,' protested Lenca.

'I can see his point and I wouldn't mind, except that—'

'Except that what?' asked Lenca as he hesitated.

'I shouldn't talk like this about him – but seeing that you're not friends any more I don't suppose it matters. I've noticed how often he disappears and does a spot of searching on his own, away from the main group. Almost as though he's looking for some other wreck.'

This confirmed her suspicions, and any doubts Lenca might have had following her discussion with Daniel were swept away in a renewed determination to

93

search for the *Valancia* herself, and in particular the Trevelyan Emerald on which he seemed to set so much store. 'You'll have to show me one day exactly what sort of work you do,' she said. 'Maybe I'll find a gold coin for myself.'

'We'll see about that.' Kip became suddenly serious. 'There's no point in trying to run before you can walk.'

'Devlyn said I did very well,' sticking out her chin and looking up at him.

'Praise indeed,' he mocked. 'Let's see how you get on with me. Are you ready?'

Apart from a few parked cars Porthoustock beach was deserted. Within minutes they had donned their gear and were walking out towards the sea.

'Try walking this way,' laughed Kip, as she stumbled in her fins and he caught her before she went headlong on to the pebbly shore.

'That's much better,' she cried, as they both turned and stepped backwards. 'Why didn't I think of it before?'

They waded out for a few yards and then side by side swam into the deeper water. Once again Lenca experienced a thrill of exhilaration and when she saw Kip give an encouraging wave she surged ahead in pure enjoyment. Seconds later he was by her side again, pointing out the curious weeds and fish that inhabited this subaqueous world. She felt lightened in spirit; all her cares and worries evaporated as she finned her way through the green water between the waving masses of weed. Nothing else mattered except the sheer pleasure of discovering the hidden delights this different, never-ending life-cycle had to offer.

When Kip suddenly indicated that they return to shore Lenca felt a sharp stab of disappointment. Surely he did not think she had had enough already? A quick

94

look at her pressure gauge showed that she still had plenty of air, so what was the hurry? She had little choice except to follow, but immediately they broke through the silver undulating curtain of the surface she pulled out her demand valve and demanded to know why he had brought her back.

'Don't get all excited.' His face-splitting grin was in evidence again. 'We haven't finished yet.'

'Then what are you playing at? I want to go down again.'

They had reached shallower waters and were wading out towards the grey stone beach.

'I'd never have believed it,' Kip said. 'I've never seen anyone take to underwater swimming as quickly as you. You're natural.'

'Then why have you brought me out?' demanded Lenca, looking furiously up into his smiling face, her violet eyes flashing darkly.

'Because,' he said with deliberate slowness, 'you were doing so well I thought we might find a fisherman who would take us out to Shark's Fin Rock and you can look for sea-urchins. As it's such a calm day I can't see Devlyn objecting.'

'Kip!' squealed Lenca. 'What a wonderful idea!' She stepped forward, forgot about her fins, and sent them both crashing down into the ankle-deep water.

'There's gratitude for you,' he teased, when they had regained their balance and sat on the bottom helpless with laughter. 'If that's the way you treat my suggestion I shan't take you out again.'

'I'm sorry,' she gurgled, 'I was going to kiss you. It's such a super plan.'

'Then what's stopping you now?' His sepia eyes twinkled wickedly. 'We can't fall far here.'

She leaned forward and pressed a grateful kiss

95

against his cheek, feeling the sharp taste of salt on her lips.

'Is that all I get?' wryly grimacing.

'That's all. Come on, let's go and find that fisherman.' She deftly took off her fins and was half-way across the beach before Kip caught up with her. She sensed that her kiss had triggered off an awareness in this dark, ruggedly handsome man, and purposely kept her tone light as they discussed the chances of finding sea-urchins. She had enough to contend with without adding an amorous Kip to her problems.

They were fortunate in finding a boatman agreeable to taking them out. He had just returned from a fruitless morning fishing, but did not seem to mind spending more time on the lucid calm of the English Channel. They discovered his name was Mike Kelly and that he was accustomed to transporting skin-divers to the Manacles.

He dropped anchor a little way from Shark's Fin Rock and a few minutes later Lenca and Kip entered the water, the calm surface now broken by their mushrooms of expired air.

At first Lenca could see no sign at all of sea-urchins. The seabed was a dense patch of swaying laminaria weed, but no football-sized urchins Kip had assured her they would find. Then suddenly he parted the kelp with his hands and disappeared head first. Lenca watched and waited and a few seconds later he emerged with a huge purple ball of spikes, pointing down for her to follow suit. Hesitantly Lenca dived into the dense weeds and was surprised to find quite a space beneath. Her first sight of a sea-urchin was a ghostly white glow a few feet to her left. As she got closer it turned into a beautiful pinky-purple ball. She picked it up, delighted, then as she turned saw another larger one, and yet another. Each time she seemed to see bigger and bigger ones and accordingly let the smaller ones tumble back to safety.

Kip joined her, enjoying her delight and pointing out spider crabs which clung motionless to the weed. He picked one up and it contracted its legs until they disappeared. Shall we take it back? he motioned, but Lenca shook her head. She liked crab, and had been told that there was plenty of good, sweet meat in this particular type, but she hated the thought of having to kill this poor defenceless creature to satisfy their own desires.

After about fifteen minutes' exploration Kip suggested they return. This time Lenca did not object. She was more than satisfied with their afternoon's dive and was eager to discuss all they had seen.

Mike soon had them back on Porthoustock beach and expressed a willingness to take them out to the Manacles any time they desired.

'What do you think?' asked Kip once they were out of their suits and resting on the blanket he had spread out.

'It's fantastic,' answered Lenca breathlessly. 'I never imagined anything could be so beautiful. Look at this,' touching the sharp, greenish spikes of her sea-urchin. 'I didn't know they looked like this. I wish we'd taken a bag so that I could have collected more.'

'There's always another time,' he grinned. 'I'll take you whenever you like.'

'Thanks, you're a pal,' and she touched his hand briefly.

A car door slamming and the screech of tyres as they spun madly on the beach before obtaining a grip caused Lenca to turn her head. The white Alfa was instantly recognizable, and the fact that the driver was not in the best of moods was evident by the way he crashed the gears. Lenca supposed he must have been there all the time, but in her excitement she had failed to notice him. Her heart lurched uncomfortably. She was not worried on her own behalf, but hoped Kip would not get into trouble for taking her out on the Manacles.

When she looked to see whether he too had noticed Devlyn, he was lying with his hands beneath his head and his eyes closed. Lenca decided to say nothing. It could be that it was merely Lenca herself with whom Devlyn was annoyed, in which case she did not want to worry Kip unduly. It would be a pity to mar the pleasure of this delightful afternoon.

'Lie down,' he murmured, opening one eye. 'There can't be much more of this glorious sunshine left. Let's make the most of it.'

So for the next hour Lenca and Kip lay side by side sunning themselves on Porthoustock Beach, making desultory conversation and enjoying the last of the summer sun.

At dinner Devlyn was conspicuous by his absence. Lenca, who had hoped he would not cause a scene in front of his friends, felt nothing but relief and was able to look forward to a pleasant evening with none of her earlier apprehension.

Kip began by telling them about Lenca's success as a diver. 'I've never seen anyone pick it up so quickly. She takes to the water as naturally as a mermaid.'

'Perhaps I was in a former life,' laughed Lenca. 'I certainly feel an affinity with the sea when I'm down there.'

'You'll be helping us next,' smiled Alan. 'We could do with an extra diver before the weather breaks.'

'What a wonderful idea!' Excitement stirred. He did

98

not know about her ambition to search for the Trevelyan Emerald, but the mere thought made Lenca feel heady with anticipation. 'When can I come?'

'Hang on.' Kip shook his head worriedly. 'I said you're good — but not *that* good. Experience is what counts on these dives, and you've a long way to go before you'll be ready for serious work.'

'Come off it.' Trevor joined the conversation. 'There's enough of us to see she doesn't come to harm. If Lenca wants to come, I'm all for it. How about you, Alan?'

'It's okay by me. As you say, we can easily keep an eye on her. She may even bring us luck. We could certainly do with it.'

Lenca clapped her hands together frenziedly. 'Oh, do let me come!' She looked imploringly at Kip, her violet eyes wide and the tip of her tongue running agitatedly across her lips. 'I won't be a nuisance, honestly. I'll do exactly as I'm told.'

'It's not really up to me,' said Kip slowly. 'Devlyn's running this operation. I don't know whether he'd—'

'*Please* let me.' Lenca could see he was weakening and spoke again before he finally convinced himself that he was doing wrong. 'I won't do anything I shouldn't. If you three all agree Devlyn won't be able to say anything. Oh, please say yes!'

And then they were all laughing, and Kip had agreed, and Lenca was very excited.

Not surprisingly sleep evaded her that night. She lay awake listening to the sounds of the house as it too settled down; the hoot of a distant owl and the occasional bark of a dog. Soon she would be near to the spot where Captain Edward Trevelyan's ship sank over a hundred years ago. Although she realized the chances of her discovering any actual treasure were slim, the very thought of being so close to history was enough to send exhilarating shivers up and down her spine.

She tossed this way and that until the sheets were screwed into uncomfortable hard lumps beneath her. She pulled them straight by the light of the moon which filled her room with harsh shadows. A glance at the clock showed that it was already nearly two. She sighed and decided to make herself a hot drink, realizing that if she didn't sleep soon she would be no good for diving tomorrow.

She pulled her housecoat closely round her slim form and quietly opened the door. The corridor was in darkness after the brilliant moonlight, but within a few seconds her eyes became accustomed to the gloom and she walked along, grateful for the soft carpet which padded her footsteps. Past Devlyn's door, from which there was no sound, and to the head of the stairs. Here it was much lighter. She cast a furtive glance at her grandmother's portrait, but the painted face smiled approvingly, and she moved quickly down into the hall. Once in the kitchen she closed the door and snapped on the light.

Meg was fussy about anyone in here, but Lenca felt sure that in this instance she would not object to her making a hot chocolate drink. The milk was almost boiling when the sound of the door opening softly caused Lenca to swing around apprehensively.

'Oh, it's you,' she said, on sight of Devlyn's pyjama-clad form, her hand fluttering to her mouth and her colour, which had receded at the thought of an intruder, returning to her cheeks. 'What are you doing here?'

He closed the door and leaned against it, his blond hair tousled as though he too had had difficulty in sleeping. 'When I heard footsteps pass my door I thought at first we had prowlers, but when I saw it was you I decided to follow.'

'What did you think – that I had a secret assignation with Kip?' she taunted hotly.

'I must admit the thought did cross my mind,' he folded his arms across his chest, 'after seeing you together this afternoon. Then I decided Kip was above that sort of thing.'

'Then why follow me?' she snapped.

'I guessed where you were going and as I wanted to speak to you I decided I'd join you for a cup of—'

Before he could finish, the smell of burnt milk stung their nostrils. Too late Lenca turned to see the white liquid bubbling over the side of the saucepan, browning almost immediately on the hot rings of the stove.

'Now look what you've made me do!' she accused, lifting up the pan and placing it on the drainer. 'Meg will never forgive me. You know what burnt milk smells like. It takes ages to get rid of.' She picked up a dishcloth and began dabbing ineffectually at the now blackened mass.

'Here, give it to me.' He was at her side and taking the cloth from her hand. 'You'll burn yourself like that.' He lifted the top of the stove and soaked up the milk that had seeped through into the drip tray. 'Best wait until it's cooled before we try and get the rest off. Why did you turn it so high?'

'How did I know I was going to get interrupted?' retorted Lenca, tipping the burnt milk into the sink and running cold water into the pan. 'What was it you wanted to talk to me about that couldn't wait until morning?' She was annoyed with herself for allowing this to happen, and annoyed with Devlyn for being the cause of it. Her eyes flashed angrily as she looked round at him and two spots of high colour flared in her cheeks.

'Your dive tomorrow,' he said quietly. 'I forbid it.'

Lenca's chin came up and her fingers curled into the palms of her hands. 'I'm afraid you're outvoted,' she said, 'four to one.'

'Oh no.' His head shook slightly. 'I'm the boss – and what I say goes.'

'Who told you?' demanded Lenca. If he hadn't found out until they were ready to go he might not have been able to stop her. With the men on her side she could not see him holding out for long – but here, on her own, what chance did she stand?

'No one actually told me,' he said blandly. 'Trevor and Alan were discussing it when I returned last night. I couldn't help overhearing.'

'And you told them I couldn't go?'

'I said no such thing, but I intend having a word with Kip. I thought he'd more sense.'

'Kip didn't want me to go.' Lenca couldn't let Kip take the blame for something that was her own fault. 'I had an awful job persuading him that I would be all right. But I will be, I assure you.' She turned her back and began scrubbing at the pan with a piece of wire wool. She needed something to occupy her attention before she lashed out at this overbearing man.

'So you think one dive on the Manacles qualifies you as an expert? That's another thing I want to tackle Kip about.' Devlyn was at her side, rinsing the dishcloth under the tap. His leg touched hers and she edged away in dismay. Despite all that had happened she still felt a tremor through her limbs at his touch and despised herself for her weakness.

'I think no such thing,' she snapped, 'but you must agree that I haven't done badly for a beginner, and with four of you to look after me, what harm can I come to?'

'We're not down there for pleasure,' he insisted. 'We have a job of work to do, and it doesn't allow us time to keep an eye on a novice.'

'I don't believe you.' Lenca rubbed vigorously at the saucepan, even though by now it was shining brightly. 'I think you're using it as an excuse. You're afraid I might spoil your little game.'

She heard his indrawn breath and felt his eyes upon her. 'And what is that supposed to mean?'

'You know perfectly well,' darting him an accusing look. 'Can you deny that you're not looking for Sir Edward's treasure?'

'Ah, now we have it!' He gave the semblance of a smile, although there was no humour in his voice. 'You think I'm looking for your ancestor's long-lost fortune and are determined to beat me to it.'

'And if I am?' flared Lenca defiantly, letting go of the saucepan and facing him.

His eyebrows gave a curious quirk. 'You think it's as simple as that, eh? For years no one has been able to trace the remotest shadow of the *Valancia*, yet you expect to go down there and find everything waiting for you?'

'Of course I don't. But I stand as much chance as anyone else, so why shouldn't I try?'

'Because it's not so easy,' he said softly. 'How many more times do I have to drill it into that brain of yours that the Manacles are fraught with danger?'

Lenca stood her ground. 'You dive there every day. Surely the danger's as great for you as for me?'

'I know what I'm up against. I understand them. I know which parts are more dangerous than others and how they'll react to certain weather conditions. It all adds up to experience, Lenca. You're not ready for the Manacles yet. I'm annoyed with Kip taking you this afternoon – even though the weather was the best we're likely to find. I just won't let you risk your life out there. Think what your grandfather would say if anything happened to you.'

'I see your point,' conceded Lenca, although she was by no means convinced that this was the only reason he did not want her to accompany them. 'And I suppose you're right.' There seemed no point in arguing further in face of his opposition. She couldn't see him changing his mind, no matter what was said, and she certainly wasn't going to beg him to take her. Best to let him think she had given up the idea – for the time being.

His smile of relief proved that he had no idea that Lenca was already beginning to plot her way round the situation, and when he suggested she sit down while he finish cleaning the stove and make them both a hot drink she obeyed without murmur.

No doubt he believed he had won, she thought amusedly. He would soon find out that Lenca Trevelyan was not a person to be so easily put off. She intended diving on the Manacles tomorrow, come what way.

CHAPTER SIX

NOT surprisingly Lenca overslept the next morning. On reaching the dining room she found it empty. Devlyn had obviously told Kip and the others that she would not be accompanying them after all. She smiled to herself, unperturbed. It made it all the easier to carry out her plans.

It shouldn't be too difficult diving on the Manacles. Admittedly Devlyn had warned her in the beginning never to dive alone, but with Kip yesterday it had all been so simple, so why not today? A glance through the window showed her that the weather looked no different – a cloudless blue sky, a brilliant sun, what more did she need.

She ate a skimpy breakfast of toast and tea, much to Meg's disgust, and then went straight into the library. The first thing was to find out exactly where the *Valancia* had gone down. She recalled seeing a map dramatically marked with a black ink cross. Apparently one of her forebears had discovered the ship's exact location and thoughtfully recorded it for future reference. After she had made a mental note of the nearest rock, Lenca's next job was to try and find the necessary equipment for her dive. She hoped Kip had remembered to take it out of his boot, otherwise it would be the end to her carefully laid plans.

The cellar allotted to Devlyn for his equipment was reached by a flight of stairs near the kitchen. Lenca waited until Meg was safely out of the way before venturing down, realizing only too well that the housekeeper would instantly object if she found out that

Lenca intended diving alone.

It was dark downstairs, and felt damp and cold. Lenca groped along the wall and found the switch. The sudden flickering of a fluorescent tube hurt her eyes before the whole area became clearly visible.

The stone floor was bare, but the walls had been whitewashed and various maps and diagrams were fastened at intervals. One in particular drew Lenca's attention, but if she expected to see any reference to the *Valancia* she was disappointed. It was grubby and finger-marked, as though much used, and showed the Manacles in great detail, but nothing had been added to the original print.

A large bench along one wall was spread with tools and dishes in which coins and odd-shaped pieces of metal were soaking. A small box of shinier coins stood in one corner together with the cannon balls and piece of ship's bell that the men had referred to earlier. A batch of photographs showed the sea bed in detail in relation to the objects already found. There was nothing to arouse any great interest, although Lenca could not imagine that Devlyn would leave lying around anything he might have found belonging to the *Valancia*. On the other hand he might not have discovered any of its valuables, yet she could not imagine him returning to this spot year after year if it was not worth his while. It was her belief that slowly and surely he relocated various items which had been scattered over a wide area of the sea bed and was building up a private collection which would be worth a considerable fortune when complete. And the most obvious place to keep them would be in his room, locked away from inquisitive eyes. It was pure supposition on her part, but what else could she think, taking into account all the facts that had come to light? He's after the emerald, I know, she whispered fiercely, but he mustn't find it, he mustn't. It's Grandfather's, and I want him to have it.

She had begun to think that her search for a wet suit was going to prove fruitless when she saw it folded neatly in a corner, complete with fins, face mask and everything else she would need, including the lifebelt Devlyn had insisted she wear. There was also a compressor for refilling the air bottles and she held her breath as she checked to see whether the tank she intended using was full. If not she had no idea how to go about refilling it. Luck was with her. Everything appeared to be in order. It would take more than one journey to get the equipment out to her car, but with a bit of luck Meg would still be upstairs making the beds and she could nip through the kitchen and get everything safely stowed into the boot before the housekeeper found out what was going on.

She felt like a thief in the night and her heart pounded violently as she made the last journey up the cellar steps. Carefully switching off the light, Lenca closed the door and raced outside. She had made it! Breathing heavily, she sat for a few minutes before starting the engine. She was in no fit state to drive.

Deep down inside she knew that Devlyn was right and that she had not sufficient skill to dive on the Manacles. Yet even as she concurred to his wisdom she started the engine and nosed her car along the winding drive. She had made up her mind to go out there today and nothing was going to stop her – least of all her conscience. All that she hoped now was that Mike Kelly would be available to take her. He had no idea that she was new to this game and would take it for granted that she went diving on the Manacles with her friends whenever the opportunity arose.

Fortune, it seemed, rode with Lenca every inch of

the way on this late summer morning. Although the first brightness had gone and the sun had disappeared behind a grey haze by the time she reached Port-houstock, Mike Kelly was leaning nonchalantly against his boat, smoking a pipe and gazing seaward as if he had all the time in the world to spare. He smiled as Lenca approached, his mahogany face wreathed in lines and his blue sailor's cap tilted forward at a rakish angle. 'They gone without you?' nodding his head towards the cars Lenca had noticed parked a little further along the beach.

'That's right,' she said. 'I overslept and they didn't wait. Do you think – do you think you could take me out?' She bit her lip waiting for his reply. Everything now depended on Mike.

He pushed back his cap and scratched his brow, looking up at the darkening sky. 'I don't rightly know whether I should. Weather's not so good today.'

'Oh, please,' begged Lenca. 'I shan't stay out long. Don't say I've brought my kit down for nothing.'

He glanced first at his watch and then at the sky and then back again to Lenca, while she waited apprehensively for his verdict. 'You win,' he said at length. 'But you're not to stay down long, mind. We could be in for a storm later on.'

'Thank you, Mike,' she said quickly. 'Thank you. You're a darling. I'll slip into my suit while you're getting your boat ready.'

Within minutes they were throbbing across the water. It was not the same clear bluey green it had been yesterday, but in her excitement Lenca failed to observe its appearance or the fact that as they rode further out it became less smooth.

'Help me on with my set, Mike,' she said as they neared Pen-win Rock which was where she had planned to dive. He held the air cylinder behind as she fastened the harness in the quick-release buckle. She pulled on her fins and gloves. Now she was ready.

'I'm not sure that I like you going down alone,' ventured Mike as he dropped anchor. 'It's a mite choppy out here now.'

'Don't worry, I'll be quite all right,' smiled Lenca confidently. 'Just make sure you don't go away, or I will be in trouble.' Before he had chance to argue any further she put her demand valve into her mouth and jumped overboard. Not for anything would she have admitted that she too was beginning to doubt the wisdom of her actions. She had planned this morning down to the last detail and refused to let anything stop her.

Before she had gone very far she realized that her dive was not going to be as simple as she had thought. Visibility was down to about ten feet and she found herself in a slightly luminous brown haze. It was going to be difficult to find anything in these murky depths, she decided, wishing now that she had listened to the advice of Mike Kelly. Then she consoled herself with the thought that Devlyn and his team could be no more successful. She moved slowly forward, all the time looking for anything that could remotely be connected with the wreck of the *Valancia*.

Her father had dived these very waters, she reflected, and her grandfather before him, probably walking over this self-same spot. All the various members of her family had tried unsuccessfully to discover Sir Edward's sunken treasure. She gazed about her, eager to learn all there was to know about these cavernous depths. Was it any different from when the *Valancia* sank in 1835? Had the years changed and reformed the seabed as man had the land? It was difficult to imagine it any different, but she remembered her grandfather saying how one day something could be visible and the next buried in several feet of sand. So strong must be the currents down here it hardly bore thinking about. If the storm Mike forecast broke what were her chances? Did it affect the bottom of the sea as much as the surface? She visualized the wind whipping the wave tops to a white spume and dashing them mercilessly against the rocks. Would she be buffeted and tossed down here?

Her skin crawled at the thought, then she shook her head in annoyance. She was allowing her imagination to run riot. Nothing would happen. Had Mike been unsure of the weather he would never have let her come down in the first place. Fishermen were notorious weather prophets.

Before her now the kelp looked like a miniature pine forest; broad leaves above stems thicker than a man's wrist. It did not look so inviting as it had in yesterday's green water, but Lenca decided that if there was anything to be found it would be beneath this mass of weed waving and twisting on the tide. She gradually shouldered her way through, only to find it darker than ever. Lesson number one, she thought; had she known she would have brought a torch. Various odd-shaped pieces she picked up from the bottom turned out to be no more than rocks or rotted pieces of timber which could have come from any one of the hundreds of vessels sunk in these waters.

A round, flat object which she felt sure must be a coin turned out to be a stone worn wafer-thin by the action of the seas. All in all she was very disappointed. She had hoped to find something, if only a piece of metal. To return empty-handed was to admit defeat. She picked up a spiky sea-urchin, then tossed it back dejectedly. A huge turbot nuzzled at her air bottle in search of food, but she glared at him in disgust and he went away. A glance at her pressure gauge showed that she had only a few more minutes' air left, and it was with reluctance that she prepared to return to the surface.

She edged her way through the thick stalks, but before she was clear of the fronds she felt a sudden tug on her air hose. She looked behind, but could see nothing – yet something was stopping her from moving. Raising her hand, she traced one of the thick laminaria stems caught between her hose and the back of her neck. How it had got there she did not know, but no matter how she pulled or twisted she could not free herself. She was stuck fast – here on the seabed – with no one to help or even to know that she was in trouble until Mike raised the alarm.

In that moment of realization it seemed to Lenca that her heart stopped beating. She felt cold and clammy and every pulse and nerve began pounding at a most alarming rate. Her throat contracted and she took in great gulps of air, her breast heaving rapidly beneath the shiny black of her suit. It was terrifying, claustrophobic. Any minute now, she thought, I shall pass out. It will be the end. Oh, why didn't I listen? My grandfather, Devlyn, Mike – they all warned me. Why was I so stupid as to ignore them? She was afraid to glance again at her pressure valve. She closed her eyes tightly and tried to calm her jangled nerves. The more I panic, the more quickly I shall use up my air. She wriggled to and fro trying to free herself from the tenacious grasp of the kelp, but all in vain. However she contorted her limbs she could not escape.

Then miraculously she felt a hand on her arm; her eyes flew open and there in front of her was another black-suited diver. Never in all her life had Lenca been so pleased to see another human being. She glimpsed a knife and the next moment she was free of the constricting weeds. Limp with relief, she was glad of the guiding hand of her rescuer as they rose slowly to the surface.

Never before had the air tasted so sweet and fresh — and precious! Lenca filled her lungs with its goodness before turning to thank the man who had saved her from certain death. But her thanks died on her lips as she encountered the grim, tight-lipped face of Devlyn Quinn.

'What a damn fool thing to do,' he grated. 'Have you taken leave of your senses?' Steel-hard were his eyes as he looked at her through narrowed lids. 'Haven't you been warned enough?'

Unpredictable tears pricked the back of Lenca's eyes and she turned away, unable to face the accusation he had flung at her. Didn't he realize she had hardly enough strength to support herself on the now heaving surface without a full-scale argument?

A sudden swell tossed them about in the water like toy ducks and the sea boiled in white foam around the rocks that broke the surface. Deep pits opened up and filled in again with horrible gurgling noises. Lenca shuddered, recalling her grandfather's tale of such happenings. At the same time Devlyn caught her shoulder. 'Let's move. This is no place for us.'

Less than fifty yards away Mike Kelly waited. He could come no nearer because of the rocks, but to Lenca those yards might have been miles. The turbulent action of the sea dragged against her arms and legs. Every stroke was an effort. The boat seemed to get no nearer. Experienced swimmer as she was it helped her not at all against such mighty waves. They treated her with the disdain accorded a piece of matchwood.

'Come on, Lenca, you can do it.' Devlyn encouraged. 'Only a little way now.'

She flashed him an anguished look and summoned up her last ounce of strength to bring her alongside the storm-tossed boat. Ready hands pulled her in, but she had reached the limit of her endurance and collapsed limply on the bottom.

As if from a distance she heard Devlyn and Mike talking. It was too much of an effort even to listen. She lay, her eyes closed, until gradually the strength began to return to her limbs. Then she opened her eyes and sat up. What had felt like minutes must have in actual fact been seconds, for Devlyn was only just climbing into the boat. He glanced at her first to make sure she was all right and as Mike started the engine he silently took off his aqualung and fins before turning to Lenca to help her off with her own equipment.

'I'm sorry,' she said, as he sat beside her on the wooden seat. 'I should have had more sense. It was so easy with Kip yesterday that I thought—'

'You'd go it alone,' he interrupted tersely. 'I'm surprised at Mike for taking you.'

'He didn't know I wasn't experienced. It's not his fault.' She seemed to be making a habit of getting other people into trouble. 'H-how did you find me?'

'Lucky for you we were diving not far away. Alan was acting as tender and spotted Mike sitting in his boat. He knew he couldn't be fishing and as far as we knew there were no other divers on the rocks today. When he told me I decided to swim across to find out what he was doing. You can imagine how I felt when Mike told me that you were diving – alone.' His lips compressed into a thin straight line. 'Why Lenca? Why? Surely you're not so naïve as to think that you could find some of that stuff your great-great whatever he was is supposed to have lost? Or were you trying to prove that I was wrong? That you could successfully make a dive in waters where even the most experienced fear for their lives?'

Lenca glared at him defiantly. Agreed she was in the wrong and he had every right to be annoyed, but did he have to be so scathing? 'You rubbed me up the wrong way when you forbade me to dive. I don't take kindly to people talking like that. If you'd used reason I might have considered it.'

'You're not a child,' he said. 'I could expect it if you were. You're a grown woman – or at least that's what you'd say if I asked.'

'Then why not treat me as such?' flared Lenca irrationally. 'You don't forbid a woman to do something. I'd have been perfectly safe with you and Kip. What was your objection?'

'I've already told you – we have work to do.' His fingers strummed impatiently against the edge of the boat. 'We need all the fine weather without taking time off to give lessons.' He glanced up at the ominous black mantle that had obliterated the sun. 'Looks as though even that's against us now.'

As he spoke a grey curtain of rain advanced towards them, the wind-driven drops stinging their faces. Twin forks of lightning sheared through the sky and a resounding clap of thunder made Lenca huddle nearer to Devlyn for reassurance. She felt his arm about her shoulder, strong and comforting, and pressed even closer as a second and more brilliant flash cut into the sea near by.

The little boat pitched and rolled, Lenca clinging tightly both to her seat and to Devlyn. It was a nightmare journey back to shore. Every second Lenca feared they would be flung out to fight for survival in the raging sea. And she had only herself to blame. Both Mike and Devlyn were at risk because of her own selfish desires. Tears mingled with the rain coursing down her face and she stifled the sobs that swelled in her throat. Stealing a furtive glance at Devlyn, she hoped he would think it was the weather that caused her anguish. She could imagine his derision if he realized that it had taken a storm of this magnitude to bring her to her senses.

Never before had land appeared so inviting. It might look grey and sombre and depressing, and practically obliterated by driving rain, but to Lenca it was the most beautiful place on earth. Kip and the others waited on the beach, their faces drawn and anxious. As the fishing vessel drew near they waded out and helped haul her over the slippery grey stones.

Everyone was grim-faced and silent. The storm had taken them all unawares. Kip handed Lenca out of the boat, a brief smile flickering across his face and his arm supporting her as she stumbled weakly when her legs touched the ground. She was ushered into Devlyn's car before she could even think of apologizing to Mike, and still clad in his diving suit, Devlyn climbed in beside her and started the engine. So strong was the force of the rain that the wipers had little effect in clearing the windscreen. Nevertheless he cautiously edged forward across the stony beach and up the steep hill towards Trevelyan Manor.

Neither spoke during the journey. Devlyn, tight-lipped and white-faced, needed all his concentration for the road ahead, and Lenca was too shocked to speak. She realized she was lucky to be alive and all her thanks were with this man at her side. What her grandfather would say when he found out she dared not think.

There would be no more diving now. If Devlyn said nothing Daniel would surely forbid it. And all through her own foolishness in trying to do something for which she was not yet ready.

Through the gate of the Manor they went, along the curving drive, and straight to the kitchen door. Meg was rolling out pastry when Lenca entered the room, followed closely by Devlyn, with Kip, Alan and Trevor bringing up the rear.

The pin fell from her hands and crashed on to the floor. 'Good gracious me!' she gasped. 'What have you been doing? I thought you'd have taken shelter in a storm like this. Take those suits off at once – a right mess you're making in my kitchen!'

Devlyn stepped forward. 'Lenca's had a shock, Meg. I think you ought to—'

The rest of his words were lost to Lenca. She felt suddenly hot and then cold, lights flashed before her eyes and she felt herself falling – falling.

When next she opened her eyes she found herself in bed. Her clothes had been stripped off and she was dressed in one of her own nighties. A hot water bottle was tucked comfortingly by her side and as she looked round the room a shadow moved from near the door.

She closed her eyes suddenly. Devlyn was the last person she wanted to see. In her present weakened state she had no desire to be scolded for the follies of her sin. She heard the sound of a chair being drawn up at her side, felt Devlyn's hand on her arm where it lay limply across the saffron-coloured bedspread. She hadn't even the energy to pull away, so instead she opened her eyes and looked at him.

'What do you want?' she said flatly. 'If you've come to tell me what a fool I've been, you're wasting your time. I know, and I'm sorry, and I won't do it again.

Does that satisfy you?'

'Not entirely,' he said, 'but I haven't come to argue. I think you've learned your lesson.' His thumb stroked her wrist as he spoke and his eyes had lost their steely hardness. 'How are you feeling? No ill effects?'

'I'm all right,' dragging away her arm and tucking it beneath the clothes. It might have been better if he *had* argued instead of acting – almost as though he cared. He did mind, of course, but only because it would upset his plans if she lost her life. No doubt he still hoped that she would change her mind and marry him. What other way would he be able to lay claim to any of the treasure he aimed to retrieve? She tossed her head wearily, trying to tell herself that his touch meant nothing to her, that she could never again regard him as anything other than a mercenary gold-digger.

His hand was on her forehead now. 'Are you sure? You look very flushed. Meg wanted to send for the doctor, but I said to wait until we saw how you are.'

Oh, *why* did he look so worried? She closed her eyes, unable to bear the tenderness of his expression, or the anxious frown creasing his brow. Only two days ago it would have been sheer heaven to see him looking at her like this – but now she knew it was all a cover-up. He was in the wrong profession – he should have been an actor. With his ability to change his moods to suit the occasion he would go far.

'Lenca! I think maybe we *ought* to send for the doctor.'

'Oh, don't fuss,' looking straight into the blue eyes so near to her own. 'I tell you I'm perfectly all right. I don't even know what I'm doing in bed. Was it your idea?' And as a sudden thought struck her, 'Who undressed me?'

He smiled at her expression. 'Don't look so shocked.

I took your wet suit off and carried you upstairs, but Meg did the rest – wouldn't let me near you again until you were tucked up.'

Lenca breathed a sigh of relief. Thank goodness for that! It would be the last humiliating straw to think that this man had actually . . . She shook her head. It hadn't happened, so no point in thinking about it. 'Thanks anyway. I can't think what happened. I've never fainted before.'

'I'm surprised you lasted as long as you did after all you've been through,' said Devlyn. 'How long had you been stuck down there?'

'Several minutes,' confessed Lenca.

Impatiently he shook his head. 'Shall I tell you what I would have done in your position, had I been stupid enough to dive without a knife?' He waited a moment, but as Lenca appeared disinclined to answer he continued, 'I'd have unbuckled my harness and swum to the surface, leaving my set behind. The quick-release buckle is designed for just such an emergency.'

Lenca bit her lip and blinked back the tears his sharp words had caused. What an idiot he must think her! What an idiot she was! If Devlyn hadn't appeared at that precise moment she could have died – unnecessarily. Never again would she think she knew better than anyone else. And never again would she dive alone. 'I – I don't know what to say,' she stammered at last. 'I never thought, I was so petrified. I suppose I should have done – eventually.'

He quirked a cynical eyebrow. 'If it wasn't too late. I suppose this has put you off diving for good.'

'Indeed it hasn't,' asserted Lenca, although no doubt that was what he hoped. She could visualize his unease at the thought that she might be successful where he wasn't. 'As soon as the weather turns fine I want to try again – not alone, though, I assure you. I've learned my lesson in that respect.'

'Glad to hear it,' he drawled, 'but I don't know whether I shall be able to spare the time.'

'I'm not asking you,' she said. 'I don't want your help. Kip will take me.'

'Indeed he will not. Kip's very irresponsible. I told him in no uncertain terms what I thought about him taking you on the Manacles. I don't think he'll volunteer again.' Solemnly he awaited her reaction.

'We came to no harm,' protested Lenca, her violet eyes bright sparks of colour.

'Fortunately, no. But it could easily have turned out like today. Who'd have thought this morning that we'd have a storm like this? I've been coming down here many years, but this is the first time I've been taken unawares. Kip's far less experienced than me. It just isn't worth the risk.'

Lenca looked at the window as he spoke. The rain beat incessantly against the glass, the rivulets falling in shimmering cascades from the sill to the path below. 'Then I'll have to find someone else – with your approval, of course.'

He smiled grimly. 'You're really determined – like al the Trevelyans.'

'What do you mean?' glancing at him sharply. This wasn't the first time he had given the impression that he knew more about her family than she did herself.

'Daniel for one. Set his mind on something and he'll go all out to get it. But of course, I'd forgotten you don't know him as well as I do. Pity – he's a grand old man.'

'Through no fault of mine,' snapped Lenca. 'And now I am here I shall see he gets everything he wants.'

Devlyn looked amused, but said nothing. Instead he

rose and crossed to the window. With hands in his pockets he gazed out at the rain-laden sky. 'It's growing lighter in the south-east. Looks like the storm's passing.'

'Thank goodness for that! I shall never live through another one without remembering today. I was sure Mike's boat was going to capsize.'

'It would take a bit to turn one of those over, although I must confess I felt apprehensive. Did you see Mike's face, though? You'd have thought we were out for a Sunday afternoon trip.'

'I was too scared to look,' admitted Lenca. 'I must go and apologize as soon as this storm clears. I feel dreadful. He could have lost his boat – and his life.'

'He's all right. No doubt he's been in worse storms than this. Don't forget he's spent a lifetime at sea. Just be thankful that we all got back safely and leave it at that.'

'It's easy to talk, but I've got to live with this for the rest of my life. I shall never forgive myself, never.' Whether it was the after-effects of her escapade, or self-pity, Lenca did not know, but before she could control them hot tears squeezed from beneath her lashes and raced down her cheeks. With a muffled sob she buried her head in the pillow. Everything had been so promising this morning, why had it to end in near-disaster?

She had almost forgotten that Devlyn was still in the room until she felt a handkerchief being pushed into her hand, and huge, gentle fingers stroking back the damp tendrils of hair from her forehead. It was too much effort to resist and for a while she allowed him to touch her. A soothing warmth crept through her veins; she closed her eyes and relaxed. It was not until his lips touched her tear-stained cheek that she realized what she was doing. She stiffened and resolutely edged away.

He sighed and rose. 'Don't fret. You're not entirely to blame. If I hadn't refused to let you dive none of this would have happened. It's as much my fault as yours.'

This admission of guilt astounded Lenca. This was a Devlyn she had not yet met. That he could apologize for something that was not truly his fault was remarkable. Unless he was acting again. It was difficult to tell whether he was sincere or not. He had convinced her before – she must be careful that he did not do it again. 'You can't really mean that. You know very well it was my own stubbornness that caused it.'

'You're bound to feel remorse,' he said gently. 'Try and sleep now. You'll be better when you wake.'

'I'm not tired,' Lenca insisted. 'I don't know why you've put me to bed. I shall get up as soon as you've gone.'

'There you go again,' he grinned insolently. 'Why don't you admit that I know better than you?'

Lenca glared. 'Get out – before I throw something at you!'

'Only if you promise to stay in bed until dinner time at least.'

Lenca grimaced. 'Seems like I don't have much option. Very well, I promise.'

'That's a good girl, now shut your eyes and go to sleep.'

Lenca's pillow hit the door just as he'd closed it and she heard him laughing as he made his way along the corridor. Furious with herself for letting him rile her, she fetched the pillow and climbed back into bed.

Strange how wobbly her legs were, she thought. Perhaps Devlyn was right for once and she did need some sleep. If she had looked in the mirror and seen her ashen cheeks, the deep purple shadows beneath her eyes, she would have agreed even more with the wisdom of his words.

No sooner had she closed her eyes than she felt herself drifting into the world of sleep, tossed on a spiral of semi-consciousness, until released from the every day world. But dreams of nightmarish quality continued to torment her. She couldn't escape from the sea! It sucked her down deep into the bowels of the earth; a thunderous, mocking laugh following her attempts to escape. She was tossed and whirled like a bubble in a bathtub, each attempt to rise foiled by currents which dragged her mercilessly deeper and deeper. She tried to scream, but no sound came. Once she thought Devlyn had come to her rescue. She could see his face, reassuring, kind, even feel his hand holding hers, guiding her, leading her – and then as suddenly as he appeared he had gone. She was alone again in this watery world, this alien world, totally unable to defend herself. Fish large and small gazed at her with glassy eyes before passing solemnly by. And then she was before Neptune himself. He sat on a coral throne and pointed his trident accusingly.

'I pronounce you guilty,' he said. 'You are sentenced to life imprisonment.'

'I'm innocent!' cried Lenca. 'I'm innocent. I didn't mean any harm – I tell you – I didn't mean it—'

The dream ended there. She woke to the echo of her own voice. Meg and a strange man stood looking down. The curtains were drawn and the electric light on. What time was it? How long had she slept? And yet she still felt tired – so tired. The faces before her disappeared in a blur. She felt a prick in her arm and heard the man's voice, 'She'll sleep properly now. You've no more need to worry. Probably be as right as rain in the morning.' And she remembered thinking, but I don't want to sleep – I've slept all afternoon. Please let me wake. I'm afraid.

But this time her sleep was untroubled. She knew not that her bedside was constantly attended, that Devlyn and Kip, even Alan and Trevor, took it in turns to sit with her in case she awoke; that Devlyn's face wore a constant worried frown and that when she had not woken by midnight he brought a blanket into her room and curled on a chair, in case she woke or called out.

The room was empty when Lenca next opened her eyes. Early morning sun slanted into her room; the sky was a tropical blue in complete contrast to the heavy blackness that had threatened their safety yesterday. She sat up and reached for her watch just as Meg popped her head round the door.

As soon as she saw that Lenca was awake she bustled straight over to the bed. 'You've had us all fair worried. How do you feel?'

'Great,' Lenca smiled, 'absolutely wonderful. Why did you call in the doctor? I'm not ill.'

'You were wandering. All about the sea – said you were drowning and couldn't escape. Master Devlyn never left your side. Poor man, he thought it was all his fault.'

'Devlyn!' Lenca looked at the housekeeper sharply. 'He was here? While I was asleep?' And when Meg nodded, 'Then it wasn't a dream that I saw his face. I felt him holding my hand, but I thought – I thought I was dreaming. Why did he do it, Meg?'

She shrugged and gave Lenca a shrewd look. 'Because he wanted to, I guess. Well, I'm certainly glad you've improved this morning. What would you liked for breakfast? Boiled egg? Poached fish?'

Lenca laughed. 'I'm not an invalid! I'll come down.

I rather fancy bacon and egg, I'm starving.'

Meg looked doubtful. 'Master Devlyn says you're to stay here until he returns.'

'To hell with Master Devlyn,' said Lenca, much to Meg's astonishment. 'I'm getting up. I've had enough bed to last me a week. I don't know why everyone's fussing – just because I got wet.'

'That's not the way I heard the story.' Meg compressed her lips and folded her arms across her ample bosom. 'Very nearly drowned, you did, and my instructions are that you stay here.'

'And I say I'm going to get up. Who's in charge here – me or Devlyn?'

'You, I guess,' Meg conceded reluctantly. 'Though what he's going to say when he returns I don't know.'

Lenca smiled. 'Let me worry about that. You go and start my breakfast. I'll be down in two shakes.'

Muttering beneath her breath, Meg left. Lenca understood how the other woman felt – Devlyn's orders were not lightly disobeyed. But she did not care. Nothing seemed so bad today.

As she dressed she made plans to visit her grandfather. 'He must be wondering why I didn't go yesterday,' she said to herself. 'I hope Devlyn hasn't told him what happened. I want him to hear my version first.'

CHAPTER SEVEN

MEG was even more doubtful about Lenca visiting her grandfather than she had been about her getting up. 'I don't like it,' she said. 'Half dying you were yesterday and now you want to drive all over there. I wish Devlyn hadn't fetched your car. Why don't you wait until he comes back? He'll take you. Though I'm sure the master won't mind you not going when he knows how ill you've been.'

'Don't exaggerate,' laughed Lenca. 'I'm not ill and I never have been. I had a nightmare, that's all.' She could have added that it was the last thing she wanted for Devlyn to take her, but she didn't. 'There's nothing wrong with me now.'

'I must admit you look well enough,' said Meg slowly. 'Oh, I suppose it will be all right. But if anything happens—'

'Nothing will happen, Meg. You're a born worrier.' Lenca hugged the housekeeper. 'I'll give you a ring when I get there. How's that?'

'It will do. But I shan't rest until you're back, and whatever Master Devlyn's going to say I don't know.' Still shaking her head, she left Lenca to finish her breakfast.

Anyone would think Devlyn was one of the family, the way Meg went on about him, thought Lenca disgustedly. No one seemed to realize that it was all a part he was playing. No one but herself. And there was nothing she could do about it – at the moment. But she would – in time. She *must*, if only for her grandfather's sake. Devlyn must not be allowed to carry on this masquerade for much longer.

All the way to the hospital Lenca racked her brains for a solution to her problem, but was no nearer an answer when she arrived. As promised she telephoned Meg and then hurried along to her grandfather's private room. As she pushed open the door she heard the murmur of voices, but too late to turn back, she carried on into the room.

Grey and blue eyes stared accusingly. Devlyn spoke first. 'Why aren't you in bed? Didn't Meg tell you that I'd left instructions for you to stay there until I got back?'

Lenca returned his gaze, trying not to show the anger his words aroused. It was strange that Meg hadn't mentioned he was here – unless she hadn't known. 'Yes – but I don't see why I should when I'm feeling perfectly all right. You're not my keeper.'

Daniel looked at his granddaughter sharply, but said nothing. Lenca sensed that he was enjoying the situation and awaited Devlyn's reply with more than a little interest.

'Neither are you a child,' came the retort. 'So it's about time you stopped behaving like one. I was just telling your grandfather what a fright you gave us yesterday, and now you come walking in as though nothing had happened!'

Lenca glared at him. 'It would take more than a soaking to keep me in bed. I told you I'm stronger than I look.' She glanced at her grandfather for support, but he was looking at Devlyn, an amused twinkle in his eyes. 'Grandfather, are you going to allow this man to speak to me like this? When I need his advice I'll ask for it!'

Daniel took her hand and drew her towards him. 'He's acting in your best interests, Helenca – knows I'd have said the same had I been there.'

'But you weren't, and I resent his treating me like — like a juvenile.'

'No, lass, he's doing what he knows I would want him to do under the circumstances. You'd best listen.'

Lenca stamped her foot. They were both against her. Devlyn had certainly won his way through, and unless she had actual proof that he was trying to double cross the older man there was little chance of her convincing him otherwise. But how could she obtain proof? Devlyn was too clever to reveal the true purpose of his visits. Only she herself knew that the work on the *Leeuw* was a façade behind which to hide. The other men had admitted that he sometimes disappeared while on a dive, but Lenca was sure they had no idea of the real reason behind his actions.

'Why should I?' she argued. '*You* might be fond of him, but he means nothing to me, and I don't see why I should have to do what he says.'

Devlyn's eyes narrowed and for one brief moment Lenca thought that he actually looked hurt. She shook her head. It was impossible. He had no real affection for her. His only interest lay in what he stood to gain. He had convinced her grandfather that she was the only girl for him, and she had been almost sure herself — once. But now she knew the real reason behind his proposal she wanted nothing more to do with the man. The sooner the weather prevented any more diving the better. Perhaps then he would go and leave them in peace.

Daniel stroked the back of her hand, his lined brown fingers surprisingly soft. He looked at her reproachfully. 'You can't really mean that? You must have given Devlyn some encouragement, or he wouldn't have asked you to marry him. You speak almost as though you hate him now. Has something gone on between you that I know nothing about?'

'Of course not,' cut in Devlyn before Lenca had time to answer. 'She's suffering from shock, that's all. She ought never to have come out.'

Because of her grandfather Lenca bit back the hasty retort that sprang to her lips, shooting him a resentful glance instead.

'I'm inclined to agree with you,' said Daniel. 'I've never heard her speak like this before.' He looked at his granddaughter closely. 'Sit down, child. This escapade of yours seems to be more serious than I thought. What made you go out on your own? I thought Devlyn was giving you lessons.' He looked again at his young friend. 'Didn't you warn her about the folly of diving alone?'

'Of course, but as you can see she takes little notice of me. She has a mind of her own.'

'So it appears,' said Daniel grimly. 'Well, young lady, what have you to say for yourself?'

'I – I thought I would be all right.' Lenca avoided the two pairs of censuring eyes. 'Kip took me on the Manacles the day before – and it all seemed so easy.' And then more defiantly, 'How was I to know the weather would change?'

'It isn't the weather I'm concerned about.' Daniel eyed his granddaughter sternly. 'It's the fact that you disregarded Devlyn's advice – and could have lost your life. And who's this Kip? Why weren't you with Devlyn?'

'Kip's one of my team,' said Devlyn. 'You remember I asked whether they could stay at the Manor?'

'Yes, yes,' irritably, 'but what was he doing with Lenca? I trust her to no one but you – you know that.'

'*I* asked Kip to take me,' Lenca said quietly. 'Devlyn

128

didn't know about it. I – he – was too busy.' She had almost said she did not want to go with Devlyn, but that would have meant more explanations. And what could she say? He would never believe anything against Devlyn. So she had little alternative but to take the blame herself.

Devlyn raised his brows and for one moment Lenca thought he was going to deny her statement, but when Daniel asked if this was true he nodded. 'I should have found time to take her, I know. But you know what it's like when the weather's fine.'

Why was he saying this? thought Lenca. Why didn't he admit that she had never asked? It was unlike Devlyn to risk being in her grandfather's bad books – and for her sake too. What was he trying to do?

Her grandfather nodded. 'True. We have precious little good diving weather at this time of the year. I don't blame you, Devlyn, it's this headstrong granddaughter of mine who's the trouble.' But he looked fondly at her as he spoke. 'I want you to promise never to go diving alone again. And you, Devlyn, I want you to keep an eye on her.'

Lenca gritted her teeth as Devlyn suddenly grinned at the older man. 'Trust me, Daniel. I'll watch her like a hawk. Any more diving will be under my strict supervision.'

Daniel looked relieved, but tired. It would have been better had he never learned of the incident, thought Lenca, and she hoped it wouldn't retard his recovery. She was so looking forward to his homecoming. If he had a relapse now she would never forgive herself.

In the car park outside the hospital Devlyn paused. 'Do you feel up to driving home, or can I give you a lift? We can always fetch your car later.'

'I'll drive myself,' replied Lenca coolly. 'I still have

to thank you for collecting it from Porthoustock.'

'Think nothing of it,' he returned airily. 'You don't really look well enough to drive, but I ought to have known you'd reject my suggestion.' He walked towards his car. 'Be seeing you.'

He doesn't really care how I feel, grumbled Lenca, as he disappeared from sight, or he'd have driven behind and made sure I got home all right. Shows how little his promise to Grandfather means!

When Lenca went down to breakfast the next morning she was surprised to find only Devlyn at the table. There was evidence that Kip and his friends had eaten, but no sign of the men. Lenca presumed they had already gone diving as the day had dawned as perfect as any she had yet known in this part of the country. So why hadn't Devlyn gone with them?

He jumped up and pulled out her chair. 'Good morning, Lenca. How do you feel today?' His voice was perfectly normal, but Lenca felt suspicious. If he had remained behind merely to carry out her grandfather's wishes wasn't this taking things too far? He couldn't really believe that she would venture out on her own again.

'I'm fine, thank you.' She helped herself to ham and egg from beneath the covered silver dishes, aware of his close scrutiny as she sprinkled them with salt.

'Do you feel up to diving again?'

Her violet eyes widened as she looked up sharply. 'What do you mean?' He couldn't be serious after what had happened yesterday.

'If you wish, I'll take you. You've obviously suffered no ill effects, so I think you ought to try again before you lose your nerve.'

'You don't have to offer,' said Lenca. 'I know Grandfather made you promise to look after me, but I shan't try anything foolish again. Don't let me keep you from your work.'

He smiled briefly. 'Don't worry, you won't. I thought you might like to dive with us.'

Lenca gasped, 'You said you had no time for novices!'

'Let's say I've changed my mind. You're not such a bad diver after all, but if you do get into trouble I'd rather you were near enough for us to help.'

Lenca had convinced herself that he was against her diving near his site for the simple reason that she might see something he had missed, so what motivated his offer now? Whatever the reason there was no point in dwelling on it; it was too good an opportunity to refuse.

'Okay,' she said at last, 'I'll come,' but she couldn't resist adding, 'if you're not afraid I might see something I shouldn't.'

His eyes twinkled. 'You still think I'm diving on the wreck of the *Valancia*, don't you? You'll see for yourself how wrong you are. There's nothing down there that even remotely resembles any part of the barque Sir Edward captained.'

'Because you've looked?' accused Lenca.

'Naturally. Who wouldn't, once they knew the story?'

'And you found nothing?'

'Nothing of interest,' he said, after a lengthy pause during which Lenca felt sure he was deciding exactly how much to tell her. But before she had time to question him further he stood up. 'If you've had enough breakfast we'd best get going. I told the others we wouldn't be long.'

Lenca had only toyed with her food after learning that she was to accompany Devlyn and now rose quickly.

As she changed into the pale green swimsuit she had worn the first time Devlyn took her diving, Lenca's heart pounded at the thought of what lay ahead. Who knew what she might discover? Admittedly she hadn't a trained eye like the others, but that didn't deter her from being every bit as keen. If there was treasure trove she owed it to her grandfather, as a member of the Trevelyan family, to do her best to find it.

Lenca's cheeks were flushed and her eyes sparkling when she rejoined Devlyn in his car. 'Don't be too optimistic,' he said. 'We spend days down there without finding a thing.'

'I'm not, I'm not,' replied Lenca, trying to convince herself as much as him that she wasn't excited.

'Then why the starry-eyed expression? I can't believe it's for my benefit.'

In her enthusiasm Lenca had almost forgotten that she hated Devlyn, but now some of her pleasure was taken out of the occasion. Her lips tightened as she said, 'No, it's not you. It's just the thought of diving again.'

He sighed. 'I might have guessed, though what I've done to merit your disapproval I can't imagine.'

For the rest of the short journey they were silent. Lenca's thoughts ran ahead to the forthcoming dive, but judging by Devlyn's face, she felt he must still be trying to puzzle out why she had suddenly turned against him. It shouldn't take much working out with a mind like his, she thought, but she had no intention of enlightening him.

Kip and his friends were waiting on the beach, already kitted up and ready to go. It took Lenca and Devlyn but a few minutes to put on their suits and they were soon in the boat heading out towards the Manacles.

'I'm surprised Devlyn has allowed you to come,'

said Kip, who had contrived to sit next to Lenca. 'After the way he rated me I thought he'd never let you dive again. Are you sure you're fit enough?'

'Gosh, yes, I'm perfectly all right. I don't know why everyone fusses.'

'If you'd seen yourself when you came in after the storm you wouldn't ask. You looked as near to death as it's possible for anyone to look. I feel it's all my fault.'

'Don't be silly.' Lenca laid her hand lightly on Kip's. 'It had nothing to do with you. It was my own decision, so if anyone's to blame it's myself.' She gave a half smile. 'I shan't do it again, don't you worry.'

Suddenly aware that Devlyn was watching them, a curiously withdrawn expression darkening his face, Lenca withdrew her hand and turned to Alan who was seated on her other side.

'Do you think we'll find anything today?'

'That's anyone's guess,' he smiled. 'Let's hope you bring us luck. We've never had a woman on the dive before.'

After they dropped anchor Devlyn suggested he and Lenca went first and the other three afterwards.

With only a moment's hesitation Lenca jumped. It was light down below and the sea a pale grey all around them – in direct contrast to the gloom of her solitary dive two days ago. She had half expected to feel afraid and was relieved when she experienced again the curious thrill that this fascinating world evoked. A silent world inhabited by glassy-eyed fish; an ever-changing world, a dangerous world!

A few moments after starting down she was conscious that her hatred of Devlyn had evaporated. It was funny that here underwater she couldn't stay cross with him. The different atmosphere calmed and soothed her nerves until she felt at peace. There was no room now in her mind for hatred. She was only aware of the thrill of adventure; of this her first real dive on a shipwreck; and that Devlyn had volunteered to take her . . .

She had tried to puzzle out the reason for his change of mind, but suddenly it didn't matter any more. They were here, together, doing something they both enjoyed. The only difference was that his objective was purely selfish, whereas she had her grandfather's interests at heart.

They reached the bottom and Devlyn produced a large-scale map, drawn on plastic paper, of the particular area they were searching. He pointed out where they had found various artefacts, showing her the markers on the seabed where they had actually been located. Some of the markers were missing and occasionally he would make alterations to the map. Lenca presumed that the violent storm had created as much havoc down here as on the surface.

She was surprised at the efficiency with which the search was carried out. In her ignorance she had expected them to move to and fro, picking up objects at random with none of this meticulous marking and recording of everything found – whether it was an important discovery like the piece of the *Leeuw*'s bell, or a relatively unimportant wrought iron nail.

The area was covered in boulders and weed and was close to the Pen-win rock – little more than twenty-five yards from where Lenca had made her unsuccessful dive.

Devlyn took photographs of the altered terrain and Lenca followed as he finned a few yards away. She had no intention of letting him out of sight – if he found anything she wanted to be there. Suddenly he swooped and picked up a triangular-shaped piece of metal. On examination it turned out to be the vital missing part of the *Leeuw*'s bell.

Lenca sifted through the sand and gravel with an unwarranted urgency after that, not noticing that Devlyn had paused to watch her frantic efforts. She hoped that this dive would prove lucky – not only as far as the *Leeuw* was concerned, but the *Valancia* as well. But eventually she was forced to admit defeat, and when Devlyn signalled they return to the surface she had no regrets.

The men themselves were delighted with Devlyn's find, for this was the conclusive missing link that the wreck was indeed the *Leeuw*. Underneath the layer of sea growth were clearly visible the letters of its name, and it was passed almost reverently from one to the other.

'Well, you can't say you didn't bring us luck,' smiled Alan. 'I vote we take you on every dive. What say you, Devlyn?'

'Not a bad idea,' he drawled, although Lenca could not help but notice the way he hesitated before speaking. He couldn't very well say in front of the others that he did not want her down there all the time, suspicious of every move he made, but she knew that these thoughts were running through his mind. 'Would you like to come?'

For a moment she was too surprised to speak. Everything he had done today had amazed her. First the invitation to accompany them on this trip, his friendly attitude which was all the more surprising in view of the way she had treated him, and now this! Then suddenly she smiled and nodded. 'I'd love to. If you're sure I won't be in the way?'

'I don't think so.' Devlyn smiled too. 'I admit I misjudged you, but now I'm inclined to think you might be an asset. Sometimes we have to squeeze through narrow places where your slim body would be a definite advantage.'

As he spoke he eyed her appraisingly and although covered completely by her black wet-suit Lenca went warm at the idea and a delicate flush coloured her cheeks. Damn the man, she thought. He still had the power to disturb her even though she despised his contriving mind. If the sea had this mellowing effect it might be best if she kept away, otherwise before she knew it she would again fall under the spell of this blond giant's undoubted charm.

'Hear, hear,' echoed Kip, and Lenca was uncomfortably aware of the amusement of the rest of the team. Her blushes had not gone unnoticed and it took little imagination to know what they were thinking. Apart from Kip, they knew nothing about the friction that existed between her and Devlyn.

'That's settled,' concluded Devlyn. 'From now on you're one of us.'

The other three jumped overboard after that and Lenca was alone with Devlyn. Around them the sea shimmered in a million different lights as the wind wafted its way across the surface. The sun was hot on her face and she was intensely aware of the man seated only a few feet away. The Manacles reared up beside them like giant sharks, waiting. Waiting for what? she wondered. Further victims? Despite the warmth of the sun she shivered. It was not a place to let one's imagination run riot, nor a place for the nerveless. In fact it seemed a most inhospitable place.

'Coffee?'

She felt Devlyn's hand on her arm. He had produced a flask and was holding a steaming cup towards her. Gratefully she accepted. The hot liquid coursed through her veins and all at once she felt better.

'I've never drunk a toast in coffee before,' said Devlyn. 'But here's to your joining our team. May it be a profitable association.' An enigmatic gleam darkened his eyes as his cup touched hers and Lenca frowned, fully aware of the meaning behind his words, but not wishing to cause a further argument by accusing him of using her for his own ends.

'Let's hope so,' she replied. 'I'm looking forward to my first find. I must confess I was a little disappointed – I thought there would be stuff all over the place just waiting to be found.'

Devlyn laughed. 'Don't forget the *Leeuw* sank in 1721. Salvage attempts were made at the time by professional Dutch salvagemen, but according to reports they didn't find much. It would seem that the local amateurs beat them to it.'

'Then why are you bothering? How do you know there's anything left worth salvaging?' It seemed to Lenca that this was still further proof that this wreck was only being used as a front.

'I would say it's virtually impossible to re-locate absolutely everything that belonged to a certain ship. There's almost always something still left to be found. Take this bell, for instance.' He picked up the fragment he had discovered, turning it over and tracing the outline of its name with the tip of his finger. 'Finding this last piece has been worth all the trouble. And now I have proof I shall certainly instigate a wider search. I find delving back into history like this absolutely fascinating.'

He sounded convincing, thought Lenca. If she didn't know better it would be difficult to believe that he was talking like this for her benefit, that all the while it was only the *Valancia* he was interested in.

'It makes you wonder,' she said, looking round at the

calm water spreading away on all sides, 'on a day like this, how a ship could run into these rocks. I mean, they're fairly close in to shore. I can't imagine any captain being near enough not to realize the danger and steering away before he got into trouble.'

'In theory, that's true,' said Devlyn, putting down his empty cup and pulling out a plastic luncheon box. 'But don't forget to take into account the weather. Remember Sir Edward setting out from Falmouth?' He pointed in the general direction of the town. 'He knew this area like the back of his hand, yet when the seas decided to take him off course there was nothing he could do about it.'

Lenca nodded. 'It's strange how one day it can be so calm and the next so turbulent. It's as though the sea is angry with someone and wants to take vengeance.' She accepted a sandwich and chewed thoughtfully for a minute. 'I dreamt the other day that it sucked me down. I don't know how far I went, but I saw Neptune and he sentenced me to life imprisonment beneath the sea.'

'Ah!' Devlyn's face lit up as though something that had been puzzling him had been solved. 'That would be when you proclaimed your innocence?'

'I – I think so – but how did you know?'

'Meg told me. She was very puzzled – couldn't think what you meant.'

Lenca smiled. 'Well, now you can tell her. Did she think it was my dark and murky past coming to light?'

'I hardly think so. I doubt if you've done a bad deed in your life.'

Lenca raised her brows. 'You sound very sure. How do you know I'm not a criminal on the run?'

'You couldn't deceive anyone,' laughed Devlyn. 'You're as open as a book. Why, I even know what you think about me.'

Was she so transparent? How could he be so sure of her feelings when she was not at all clear herself? 'You amaze me,' she said. 'If you're so positive, how about telling me? I should be interested to find out whether you're right.'

'You wouldn't admit it, if I was,' scoffed Devlyn. 'No one likes to feel that their innermost thoughts are no secret. One day I'll find out whether what I think is true – then I'll let you know.' He pressed the lid back on to the sandwich box. 'Say, would you like to come out for a drink tonight? I know a nice cosy pub not far away.'

Had he forgotten she no longer wanted his friend-ship? Admittedly since her accident things had been different between them. The hatred she had felt when finding out that he knew about her ancestor's will had lessened, but she still distrusted him. He had no real affection for her – his only interest lay in being able to establish a rightful claim to the Trevelyan fortune. She sighed deeply. 'If you're so clever you'll know that I have no wish to go anywhere with you.'

Devlyn spread his hands expressively. 'You're here now.'

'This is different.'

'In what way?'

'Well, this is work – as far as you're concerned, and I'm finding out what you do.'

Devlyn shrugged. 'And I thought I was making pro-gress. So the answer's no?'

He looked so disappointed that Lenca hesitated. Something inside urged her to accept. Something she couldn't understand. *Go on*, seemed to say an inner voice. He won't be here much longer after all. Enjoy yourself while you can. It can't do any harm. 'Maybe I will,' she said at last. 'But don't get the wrong idea. Things haven't altered between us.'

'You mean you still resent me — for some curious reason of your own?' He slid along the seat until his arm was almost touching hers. 'I love you, Lenca. *I* haven't changed. I don't know what I've done to merit your disapproval, but—'

The other men were surfacing! Lenca could see their bubbles and the colour of their yellow air bottles flickering way down in the depths, and their orange hoods making streaks of colour in the pale green water. She felt relief that their conversation had been brought to a premature end and rose abruptly, watching as they popped up side by side. Devlyn muttered something under his breath that she was unable to hear, but Lenca concentrated on the men uncoupling their harness.

'Look what we've found!' exclaimed Alan as soon as he had taken off his face mask. He revealed a handful of silver ducatoons, and in the general excitement that followed Lenca forgot for a while Devlyn's declaration of love.

It was not until she was getting ready for her evening out that remembrance caused her to pause in the act of brushing her hair. She hoped he would not bring the topic up again. It was embarrassing to have a man vowing he loved her, when she knew perfectly well that he did not. That if it hadn't been for the Trevelyan fortune he would probably have never given her a second thought.

That afternoon her grandfather had asked how things were between them, and it had been difficult to give him a straight answer. She wanted to tell him the truth, but knew how much it would hurt him. Although he looked much better these days she could not run the risk of his having a relapse. So instead she had said that they were friends, but that was all. He was not satisfied, she could tell, but rather than run the risk of having to recourse to lies she had left early, explaining that she had a date with Devlyn. This was perfectly true, after all, and had seemed to please Daniel so that he had settled down happily after she had gone.

Now, as she put the finishing touches to her hair, she wondered whether she had been wise in agreeing to go out with Devlyn again. There was no denying the fact that he was physically attractive, and when he wasn't being rude he was the most charming man she had ever met. She had thought she loved him – until she had discovered that he was a hypocrite – and now she did not know what to think.

He was waiting in the hall when Lenca went down. 'You look perfect,' he said, holding out a hand as she reached the last step. 'Like a woodland nymph. I'm glad you remembered I like you in green.'

'I'd forgotten you said that,' replied Lenca lightly, wishing she had chosen something different from this Lincoln green silk dress. 'It happens to be one of my favourites.'

'Then you have excellent taste,' he countered, not at all put out by Lenca's reply. 'My car's waiting. If you're ready we'll go.'

It took no more than ten minutes to reach the place Devlyn had chosen. It was a low, whitewashed, many-roomed building called the Pirate's Arms. Lenca could imagine it being used in days of old by just such people and glanced about with interest at the many curios on display.

He led her into a room which was as yet deserted, choosing a table set in the corner beside an ingle nook fireplace. 'What would you like?' he asked, as soon as she was seated.

'Brandy, please.' It was not her usual drink, but she felt in need of something stimulating. It was a little too private and cosy in here at the moment. Probably very much to Devlyn's liking, but not at all what she had expected or even desired.

As if in answer to her wishes the door opened to admit three middle-aged men, each looking as though he had spent a lifetime at sea, faces tanned to a shade of rich mahogany and loose-fitting navy sweaters worn above similar coloured trousers. They nodded cheerfully to Lenca and Devlyn as they took their seats at the next table.

Before long the room was crowded and the air filled with smoke and raised voices and an occasional guffaw of amusement.

'Happy?' Devlyn eyed her speculatively as he brought out his own pipe and filled it with tobacco.

'Yes, thanks. It fascinates me just to sit and watch.' It was the first time she had seen Devlyn smoke his pipe and the scent of tobacco reminded her of the day she had entered his room. The names Manacles and *Valancia* had been a mystery to her then. The sea had played very little part in her life before and the idea of diving for buried treasure had never entered her mind. It was strange how her whole life pattern had altered since her mother's death. She had found a grandfather she knew nothing about, had learned that the whole of her family had connections with the sea, and had met this complex man who succeeded in charming her one minute and aggravating her the next.

He was smiling now, his blue eyes crinkling kindly at the corners, and his pipe pulling down the side of his mouth. It was difficult at this moment to imagine him anything but the perfect gentleman he portrayed. It was only by continually reminding herself that he was out to swindle the Trevelyan family that she could re-frain from succumbing to his charm.

Their eyes met and held until Lenca turned away, hotly aware of the intensity of his gaze. There had been open admiration on his face and unwillingly she could feel herself responding. How can I even like such a despicable character? she thought. What's the matter with me? Have I no pride?

'It's lucky we came early,' said Devlyn. 'Or we wouldn't have found a seat. I never realized it got so crowded.'

Relieved that he had broken the tension between them, Lenca followed his gaze. The room was full now of sailors and their wives, young men on holiday with their girl-friends, and all around the conversation centred on the sea and ships. One group in particular must have been divers, observed Lenca, as she heard a voice suggest they dive on the Manacles tomorrow. 'We found a load of stuff there last year,' he went on. 'Let's see if our luck holds out again.'

'What sort of things did you find?' asked one of the girls.

'Coins, jewellery, even. Of course we had to—?'

His voice was lost, as someone shouted an order to the bar. Lenca looked at Devlyn and saw that he too had been listening. He still looked at the man in question, eyes narrowed and a thoughtful expression on his face.

'What do you think he found?' asked Lenca, feeling suddenly sure that the jewellery had belonged to the *Valancia*.

'Nothing of value, I'll be bound.'

'How can you be so sure?'

'I'd have heard. I keep in constant touch with the Receiver of Wreck. In your grandfather's interests, of course. I mean, he never bothers to check himself.'

He wouldn't be able to claim it, anyway, thought Lenca, and well you know it, but all she said was, 'I see.' She became certain of the fact that he was more concerned about this find than he admitted when on his way to get drinks he stopped to speak to the diver.

'What did he say?' she asked, as soon as he returned.

'Oh, not much,' airily. 'I merely asked where he intended diving so that we wouldn't get in each other's way.'

'You didn't ask him about the jewellery?'

'Of course not. Why should I?'

Lenca shrugged. 'I merely thought . . .'

'You didn't think it came from the *Valancia*?' He suddenly laughed, yet it was a hollow laugh and only succeeded in making Lenca more suspicous.

'Well, it might have,' she said defensively.

'You're letting the thought of your ancestor's treasure bother you too much,' he said. 'For generations now no one has succeeded in finding anything, so I think it's best if you put it right out of that enquiring little mind of yours. Whatever was down there has disappeared and unless some freak tide churns it up, or someone with enough capital and time instigates a full-time search, I can't see it ever being found again.'

'You sound very sure?' Lenca looked at him closely.

'I am sure, Lenca. Believe me, I know what I'm talking about. There've been so many disasters on the Manacles that it's difficult to determine exactly which ship your find has come from, unless you have all the details to hand, and even then we're not always right. I know you're suspicious of everything I do, but believe me, Lenca, it will be no easy task to find Edward Trevelyan's fortune, even believing that he had the stuff on board at the time.'

Lenca frowned. 'What do you mean? It said in that book that all his personal possessions went down with him.'

'I'm just trying to say,' he explained patiently, 'that you don't have to believe everything you read. Don't you think it strange that nothing at all has been found after all this time?'

'I suppose so,' said Lenca slowly. 'But you're the expert.' His statement puzzled her. It was as though he was trying to convince her that there was nothing down there after all. But why should he do that? Why? Unless he had already found it and was only waiting to get her to marry him. That must be it. There could be no other explanation.

'Now what are you thinking?' asked Devlyn. 'You're looking at me very suspiciously.'

'I was just wondering where his stuff could be if it wasn't at the bottom of the sea.'

'Your guess is as good as mine,' he said lightly, 'but enough about shipwrecks and treasure, let's talk about us.'

Lenca arched her fine brows. 'I can't see that there's much to talk about there.'

'Oh, but there is. I love you, Lenca – and at one time I thought you loved me. In fact I think you still do – even though you won't admit it. So why not tell me what's the matter? Whatever I've done I'll try and put right.'

'I'm sorry,' replied Lenca. 'I – I can't tell you.'

'But why, Lenca? Why?' He placed his strong brown hand over hers and she could sense the urgency with which he waited for her reply. She tried to pull away, but his grip tightened and whether she liked it or not her arm tingled at his touch and her heartbeats quickened.

In that moment she knew she still loved him.

'Please, let me go – you're hurting!'

His fingers immediately slackened. Swiftly she gathered up her bag and hurried out of the room. Once outside she pressed her hands to her burning face. She still loved him! There was no point in denying it. But she mustn't give in, not now. It was all a game to Devlyn. There would be no happiness married to a man whose only interest lay in the financial side of the agreement. For her own and her grandfather's sake she must deny her love; hard though it would be, no one must ever guess at the true state of her feelings.

CHAPTER EIGHT

THROUGH the thin silk of her dress Lenca felt Devlyn's hand on her shoulder. She wanted to turn and press her body close to his, feel his arms around her and hear his whispered words of love. Instead she forced herself to move away, aware of his indrawn breath at her rejection. In a voice tight with emotion he said, 'You must tell me, Lenca. I need to know. Don't you know what you're doing to me?'

If only he really meant that, thought Lenca, how happy she would be. 'We haven't known each other very long,' she said at last. 'How can you expect me to know what I think?'

'Love doesn't need thinking about,' he said harshly. 'It happens. Just as I fell in love with you – and you with me. Can you deny it? Can you deny that the day I asked you to marry me you didn't feel any love?'

'It was physical attraction,' said Lenca quickly. 'That's all. Once I'd thought things over I knew you weren't the one for me.'

'We'll see about that,' and before she could anticipate his actions Devlyn had pulled her into his arms. She could feel the lean strength of his body as he crushed her relentlessly to him. Only seconds before she had longed for this moment, but now she fought hard to free herself. There was no escape, however, he was too strong. As his face drew threateningly near she closed her eyes in a desperate attempt to shut out this – dearly beloved man. His lips touched hers, tenderly at first, and then with increasing passion as he realized she was not resisting. It was an exquisite moment of joy

147

and pain, of ecstasy and madness. She could wish for no more than to spend the rest of her days at his side, yet she knew she had to forgo this pleasure. Devlyn Quinn was acting. He did not really love her. She would be a fool to believe otherwise.

She steeled herself to remain immune, to lie passive in his arms, until at last he flung her from him. Devlyn had paled beneath his tan, his eyes searched her face as if he still could not believe that she did not care for him. then in a gesture of anguish he turned away. 'Let's go,' he said thickly.

The journey home was embarrassingly silent. Devlyn gazed ahead, tight-lipped, his actions automatic as he negotiated the curves in the road, his mind occupied by thoughts known only to himself. Lenca sat perfectly still wondering what the outcome would be. Without her he could lay no claim to the Trevelyan fortune. Did it mean so much that he should react like this? The idea was ludicrous. Yet what else could she think? He gave every indication of being a bitterly disappointed man, and this was the only conclusion she could reach.

The more she thought about it the more annoyed she became, and by the time they reached the Manor her simmering fury was on the verge of boiling over.

Had Devlyn spoken even one word things might have been different, but the fact that he completely ignored her as they entered the house was the final degradation so far as Lenca was concerned.

He had one foot on the bottom stair when she spoke.

'Do you really think I can't see through you? That I don't know what game you're playing?'

Slowly he turned, his face pale but composed. He walked deliberately towards her. 'What do you mean?' His eyes were almost grey as he stared coldly at her.

'You know very well what I'm getting at,' replied Lenca. 'Sir Edward's will.'

He frowned. 'What on earth has that to do with me?'

'Precisely nothing – but can you deny reading this?' and she produced the copy she had tucked into her handbag.

'No, of course not – but I still don't see what you're getting at.'

He didn't even look guilty, Lenca observed, and she replied hotly, 'Under the terms of this will you only get ten per cent of anything you find belonging to the *Valancia* – and Grandfather gets nothing.'

'I believe that's what it says.'

'Don't you see it would break his heart if anything was found and he couldn't claim it?' flashed Lenca.

'I don't think so,' he said airily.

'You're a heartless brute!' she returned, steeling herself from lifting her hand to strike him. She wouldn't gain anything by it at the moment. 'Have you no feelings?'

He lifted one eyebrow. 'Oh yes, I have feelings. Not that it seems to matter to some people.'

'I know exactly where your interests lie,' she said, ignoring his innuendo, 'and I can't see you risking your life for a measly ten per cent. But if you thought you could lay claim to it all – that would be different, wouldn't it?'

Devlyn's eyes narrowed at her accusing tones and he caught her wrist roughly. 'What are you getting at?'

'I don't have to tell you,' she grated. 'It's all too obvious without my explaining.'

'I don't know what you're thinking,' he said, 'but it sounds pretty insulting to me. You'd better apologize before I do something I regret.'

'You wouldn't dare,' cried Lenca. 'Let me go!' twisting in vain to free herself.

'When you say you're sorry.'

'That will be never.' Lenca's violet eyes sparked fire. 'I'll never, never, *never* say I'm sorry to you. You're the most detestable person I've ever met. You think of no one but yourself and I hate you – do you hear – I hate you! What my grandfather sees in you I'll never know.'

He smiled at that. 'You'll live to regret those words one day. You wait and see.' Abruptly he released her.

Lenca rubbed the reddened skin round her wrist. 'I don't think so,' she said haughtily. 'Please let me pass, I'm going to bed.'

He stood back at once and Lenca mounted the stairs. She felt him watching her and was relieved when she reached the privacy of her room.

As soon as the door closed hot, scalding tears slid down her cheeks. Angrily she dashed them away. Crying would solve nothing. She sat before the mirror and stared solemnly at her reflection. Her eyes were two anguished pools of colour in a ghostly face. It hurt all the more because she loved Devlyn. Perhaps she ought to have accused him outright? But what was the use? He would only have denied it. *She* knew it was true. That was enough. Tiredly she ran her fingers through her hair, allowing her head to rest in her cupped hands. The future had appeared so promising when Daniel Trevelyan first invited her to make her home with him. She had left the Midlands with a carefree heart, eagerly looking forward to her new life. Then Daniel had fallen ill on the day she arrived, and Devlyn had turned up acting as though he owned the place. 'Why did it all have to happen?' she cried. 'Aren't I going to find any happiness?'

Wearily she prepared for bed. The only consolation was that Devlyn wouldn't be here much longer. Yet memories would remain. It would take a long time to erase this peculiar love/hate relationship from her mind – if ever.

The next morning breakfast was as normal. Devlyn made no reference to their quarrel, for which Lenca was thankful as it would have led to explanations so far as the other men were concerned. Yet it irritated that he could take her accusations so calmly. When the telephone rang she was the first out of the room. It was her grandfather.

'Is anything wrong?' she asked, wondering why he was ringing so early.

'Of course not,' came the brusque reply. 'Get your car out, girl. I'm coming home.'

'Grandfather! That's wonderful. I'll be there as soon as I can.'

She raced back to tell the others, gulped down her coffee, and was back in the hall when Devlyn caught her up. 'We'll go in my car,' he said. 'It will be more comfortable.'

'Oh!' Lenca stopped. She did not relish the idea of travelling alone with him after last night. 'I didn't realize you'd want to come. Perhaps you'd best go alone. I'll get his room ready.'

A slight frown at her reaction. 'Meg will do that.'

'No, I've just remembered. It's her day off.'

Devlyn took her shoulders and looked into her face. 'Don't you think you're being ridiculous?'

'I don't know what you're talking about,' said Lenca shortly. 'Someone's got to get Grandfather's room ready.'

'It's not so important that it won't wait. He won't go straight to bed.' Then he shrugged. 'But if that's what

151

you want, I won't argue. I don't suppose he'll object to me fetching him.'

'You know very well he won't,' Lenca could not resist retorting as he turned away. 'You've made sure of that.'

He gave no indication that he had heard and she felt suddenly ashamed. She was being petty and childish. Far better to treat the whole affair with dignity.

Lenca had only guessed that it might be Meg's day off, but as it turned out it was true; although when the housekeeper found out that her beloved master was coming home she wanted to stay.

'No, no,' insisted Lenca. 'You must have your time off. Anyway,' with a pleading smile, 'I'd like to get his things ready. I haven't had chance to do much for him since I came.'

Meg relented at that, but Lenca knew that she disliked the idea of not being home when Daniel arrived, and she could foresee the housekeeper returning early.

Apart from one cursory glance when she first arrived Lenca had not seen her grandfather's room. Meg had said he liked no one touching it and now she could see why. A giant desk stood in one corner littered with papers. Books were piled on chairs. The only piece of furniture not covered by reading matter was his bed. Lenca supposed that he knew where everything was, though to her eyes it looked a hopeless mess.

She plugged in the electric blanket and switched on the fire. She vacuumed and dusted, being careful not to displace any of his papers, and then stepped back to survey the final effect. It looked no better, she thought wryly. It was a depressing room. Dark panelled walls and brown carpet did not help. What it needed was some flowers, she decided. They would brighten it up tremendously.

She collected scissors from the kitchen and cut an armful of dahlias and gladioli which grew in profusion round the side of the house. Carefully she arranged them in a cut glass vase and carried them into her grandfather's room.

'That's better,' she said aloud, moving some papers to one side and placing them on his desk. 'Much better.'

Suddenly a few words from a letter she had uncovered caught her eye. She did not mean to read it, but unable to help herself she scanned the rest of the page. It was dated January 11th.

... I have had some of the artefacts analysed and am sure now that they are part of the *Valancia*'s treasure. I will search again when I come in the summer ...

It was signed by Devlyn Quinn.

Her legs trembling, Lenca sank down on to the chair. She closed her eyes and swallowed the sudden constricting lump in her throat. 'It can't be true,' she whispered. 'Grandfather wouldn't deceive me as well.' But had he deceived her? Now she came to think about it she could not recall him actually saying he had not told Devlyn about the *Valancia*, or that Devlyn had not been searching for it. So far as she could remember he had evaded giving her a direct answer. So they were in it together. Devlyn was not the law-abiding character he tried to make out – or Daniel. The younger man was to find what he could on behalf of her grandfather and no doubt he would be handsomely rewarded. There would be no question of it being reported to the Receiver of Wreck. No wonder he had not shown any concern about the ten per cent!

And how fortunate for both of them that she had turned up. What a fool they had made of her!

Together they had contrived this – this farce of Devlyn professing to fall in love. His proposal of marriage. No wonder her grandfather had been upset when she refused. It hurt to think that he too had treated her with little regard for her own feelings.

Bitterly Lenca left the room. There was only one way out – she must leave. Her legs dragged as she climbed the stairs to her own room. To think that both the men she had learned to love had all the time been using her as a means to their own end. 'Why did I ever come here?' she whispered fiercely to the portrait of her grandmother. 'Why?' She could have been so happy. It was a beautiful house in a beautiful part of England. It would be heartbreaking to leave, but what choice had she? In the circumstances it was impossible to remain. She had a friend in Birmingham who would put her up until she found somewhere to live. Tomorrow she would go, as soon as her grandfather was settled.

She half packed her suitcase in readiness before going downstairs to await their arrival. Slowly she wandered from room to room trying to imprint every detail in her mind. Soon it would all be behind. Her joy in this house had been shortlived, but no one could take away her memories – bittersweet though they were.

Soon the sound of tyres on the drive brought her hurrying to open the door. Daniel leaned on the younger man's arm as he climbed the steps.

'Grandfather!' Lenca ran to his other side and between them they helped him into the sitting room where he sat down heavily in the leather armchair.

'A drop of whisky,' he breathed, looking at Devlyn expectantly. 'Be all right in a minute. Just a bit short of breath.'

Lenca hovered anxiously at his side, not really sure whether he should be drinking alcohol, but knowing that nothing would stop him. 'It's nice to see you home, Grandfather. I'm sorry I didn't come. I'd forgotten it was Meg's day off and I've been getting your room ready.'

'Don't fret, lass. Devlyn's explained. Ah, thank you,' taking the glass from Devlyn. After a few sips his breathing returned to normal and his cheeks which had been unnaturally pale became a healthy pink.

Dropping to her knees at his side, Lenca looked up at Daniel. It was difficult to believe that he was capable of planning deception. 'I expect you've missed your home,' she said. 'It's a lovely old place.'

'And I wasn't here to show you round,' he replied sadly. 'I'd have liked that. But never mind, we'll soon make amends.'

Lenca smiled. He was making it doubly difficult for her to stick to her decision, but she *must*. To remain would only involve more heartache.

'It's certainly been different without you,' said Devlyn. He stood with his back to the window, a glass of whisky in his hand.

Without being asked, thought Lenca grimly. Just like the day she had found him here.

'It's fortunate Lenca was here,' he continued, 'It would have been no fun otherwise.'

'Don't expect it would, my boy. She's a nice girl. Wish we'd got together years ago, eh, Lenca?'

'Yes, Grandfather,' replied Lenca dutifully.

'If it wasn't for that obstinate mother of yours we would have done.'

Devlyn smiled. 'She's got an obstinate daughter as well.'

'Don't tell me, I know.' Daniel looked at his grand-daughter fondly. 'You're a stubborn little miss when you want to be. Why won't you marry Devlyn, eh?

What have you got against him?'

Had Lenca not found Devlyn's letter she might have told him about her suspicions, but now they were both involved what could she say? She glanced at Devlyn and saw him shake his head warningly.

'Don't embarrass me, Grandfather,' she laughed. 'I can't tell you while he's here.'

'Why not? You must have given him a reason.'

'Oh yes, he knows why. Why don't you ask him?' and before he could answer. 'I'll go and see about lunch.'

She had used this as an excuse. Meg had already prepared a cold meal, but Lenca felt the need to escape, before she said something regrettable.

Daniel ate very little of the cold chicken Lenca put before him. He said he was tired and shortly afterwards Devlyn helped him to his room for a rest.

After washing up Lenca decided to finish her packing. She did not really like the idea of leaving her grandfather. He was still far from well. But she hardened her heart. He had Meg – and Devlyn. They would see he lacked for nothing.

As she took the last dress from its hanger the door opened and Devlyn came in. His eyes narrowed as he saw the open suitcase. 'What's going on?' he demanded, clearly forgetting whatever it was he had been about to say.

Annoyed that he should enter without even bothering to knock, Lenca glared. 'Isn't it obvious? I'm leaving.'

'I can see that, but why? If it's because of me, forget it. Your grandfather needs you far more than I do.'

'You think so? He managed perfectly well before I came, so why not now?' She knew she sounded callous, but this was the way it had to be. There was no room left in her heart for sentimentality.

'He's a sick man, Lenca. Have you forgotten?'

'No,' softly now, 'but he's getting better. Meg will look after him.'

Devlyn looked at her gravely. 'There's something I think you should know. Sit down.' He motioned to the bed and as she looked questioningly at him he sat beside her.

'What is it?' she said. 'Grandfather *is* going to get better?'

'I'm afraid not,' sadly shaking his head. 'He hasn't got much longer – no, wait. He knows, and he's accepted it, but I think you ought to be here.'

Lenca stared at Devlyn for a full minute before her face crumpled and uncontrollable sobs shook her body. She mutely accepted his handkerchief and did not resist when she felt herself being drawn into his arms. In that moment she drew strength from his presence and clung to him like a child would her father.

'I – I never realized,' she said at last, her voice thick and unsteady. 'Poor Grandfather, he – he's so brave.'

'One of the best,' added Devlyn. 'He didn't want you to know – but I had no choice.'

'I'm glad you told me.' Lenca gave a watery smile. I'd never have forgiven myself if I'd left now.'

'I knew you'd feel like that.' He released her and crossed to the window. He was silent for a few moments before saying, 'There's something else I want to tell you.'

'Not more bad news?' Lenca felt she could stand no more on this day of days.

His lips flickered in a brief smile. 'It depends which way you look at it. Last year I found some – some gold plate and a few silver spoons which I subsequently discovered belonged to the *Valancia*. Your grandfather

157

knows about these, and because I'm – well, who I am, he can't claim them, neither unfortunately can I. Daniel asked me then if I'd try and find the Trevelyan Emerald. He knew he could never own it, but thought if he could have it for a little while before he handed it over to the authorities he would be happy.' He sighed and studied his fingernails as though they were of primary importance. 'It looks as though he'll never see it, but – well, now you know why I'm here.'

'I see.' It helped to know that he was searching for the *Valancia*'s treasure with her grandfather's approval, but it still did not alter the fact that he had tried to entice her into marriage so that he could legally claim anything he found.

'I'd like to be alone now,' she said at length. 'I've got much to think over.'

'Of course.' His hand rested on her shoulder. 'Don't upset yourself too much. Daniel mustn't know I've told you.'

Her skin burned at his touch and she felt herself quiver with excitement. It surprised her that even in this moment of sorrow he should still have the power to disturb her, and she despised herself for it. It was going to be hell staying here, knowing him for what he was – and knowing that her love was doomed. She had always imagined love as being wonderful and stimulating, something to be shared quite frankly, with no inhibitions, no stubborn pride. The consummation of all hopes and dreams. Never had she envisaged it to be a one-sided affair. Her preconceived lover had been a step above all others, and it was painful now to realize that she had fallen for a man who put worldly goods before personal happiness.

He must have told her about his arrangement with her grandfather to try and soften her, to make her see him in a kinder light. He could not know that she was more deeply hurt by his asking her to marry him so that he could get his hands on her grandfather's considerable fortune than she had been when she suspected him of trying to swindle Daniel.

Bitterly she clenched and unclenched her fists. She could see no way of leaving now, she must do all she could to make her grandfather happy. These next few weeks would be precious to him and she must do nothing to mar his pleasure. It was all the more tragic that it should happen now. They had such a lot to discuss. Twenty years is a long time. There was so much she wanted to know, and he in his turn would want to hear all about her childhood. He had missed his rightful inheritance of seeing his granddaughter grow up and it was only right that she should tell him all she could remember.

Slowly Lenca re-hung her dresses in the wardrobe. Her movements were automatic. Devlyn's news had numbed her senses. She knew she must pull herself together and not give Daniel the slightest hint that she was aware of his illness. Meg too must not guess, or she would be unable to hide her grief. The housekeeper was an open, honest soul with a capacity for deep and genuine affection, and Lenca knew it would be the end of her world when her master was gone.

Continually throughout the afternoon Lenca kept a close watch on her grandfather, almost afraid to leave the house. Each time she looked in he was sleeping soundly – until early evening when Meg had returned and dinner was being prepared. He smiled when his granddaughter entered the room.

'There you are, girl. I feel better now. What time is it?'

'Nearly six,' said Lenca.

'Good gracious, I must get up. Send Devlyn to help me get dressed. Can't manage these confounded buttons myself. My fingers are all thumbs.'

'Why don't you stay here?' Lenca's voice was softly persuasive. 'I'll bring you a tray.'

'Why on earth should I?' His bushy grey brows shot up. 'I've had enough bed in that place. Well, are you going or do you want to help me yourself?'

'I'll fetch Devlyn.' He certainly didn't act as though he was ill, thought Lenca admiringly.

She found Devlyn talking to Kip in the sitting room and told him what was wanted.

'I'm looking forward to meeting your grandfather,' said Kip after he had gone. 'He sounds quite a character, from all I've heard.'

'He is that,' answered Lenca, relaxing into a chair opposite Kip. 'He has a mind of his own and a way of getting what he wants. I asked him to stay in bed now, but he wouldn't. He's still not well and I rather think the journey taxed him more than he realizes.' It was easier than she had expected to speak naturally about her grandfather. Probably because he didn't look ill, she thought.

'Old people are usually stubborn,' he said kindly, 'but I expect he's curious about the folks who've invaded his house while he's been away.'

'Of course, I'd forgotten he hasn't met any of you. Should be quite a pleasant evening. What success have you had today?'

Kip shook his head ruefully. 'None at all. I hope now your grandfather's home it doesn't mean you won't come diving again? We need your luck, and it seems to be the only time I see anything of you.'

'I shall come,' said Lenca, 'you can depend on that.'

'How are things between you and Devlyn these days?'

He watched closely as Lenca pondered her reply. 'We're not exactly what you'd call the best of friends,' she said at last. 'I still have reservations – but—'

'You can't help liking him – is that it?'

'Something like that,' smiling wryly.

'In fact,' Kip nodded wisely, 'I'd go so far as to say that you're more than a little in love with him.'

Lenca shot him a startled glance. 'What makes you say that?'

'Pure and simple observation. I've seen the way you react – the way you look at him when you think no one's watching. I'm very fond of you myself, Lenca, and that makes me more perceptive to your moods than, say, Alan or Trevor.'

'I didn't realize it was so obvious,' said Lenca. 'I shall have to watch myself. He must never guess the way I feel.'

They were silent for a moment after that, each engrossed in their own thoughts.

'Kip,' said Lenca eventually, 'is it possible to love and hate someone at the same time?'

'Phew!' he breathed. 'You don't ask easy questions, and not knowing the full facts I can't really give you a proper answer.' He studied the ceiling, his eyes narrowed in thought. After a few minutes he spoke again. 'There are many different kinds of hatred, just as there are love. We both know the type of love a woman feels for a man, so all we have to do now is analyse your hatred.'

'Sounds simple put like that,' smiled Lenca.

'Let's see now,' he said, 'there's revulsion, nausea – but you don't feel either of those. There's resentment – is that what you feel?'

Lenca shook her head. 'I don't think so. I did in the beginning, but not now.'

'Then there's distrust – you distrust him, I know, but I don't think that's enough.' Suddenly he sat forward. 'Disillusionment – that's it! He hasn't risen to your ideals and coupled with your suspicions it makes you feel this hatred. Am I right?'

Lenca nodded. 'Mmm, I think so. Sounds stupid and trivial when you put it like that.'

'No, no, it's a natural reaction. All you've got to do now is find out whether you really have ground for your doubts. Once you've established that you'll go either one way or the other.'

'That's easier said than done. Apart from asking him outright I don't see what else I can do.'

'Then ask him.' Kip rose and looked down into Lenca's troubled face. 'You'll never be happy until you know.'

'I suppose you're right.' Lenca grimaced; it wasn't a task she relished.

'Of course I am, though I must be a fool to even suggest it. Once you and Devlyn settle your differences there'll be no chance for me at all.'

'Kip, I'm sorry.' Lenca pulled herself up beside him.

'I know,' he said. 'It's all right, I think I've known from the start that there was no hope. The day I saw Devlyn bawling you out of his room I knew there was something between you.'

'Heavens! How did you figure that out?'

'Call it intuition,' he smiled. 'It's not only women who have it.'

The entrance of Alan and Trevor, followed by Devlyn and her grandfather, put a stop to further private conversation.

Daniel was very interested in the men's accounts of their diving experiences and regaled them with stories of his own boyhood. Altogether it was a very lively evening and no one looking at her grandfather, thought Lenca, could guess the torment he must be feeling. He was a very courageous man and she admired him greatly, despite the fact that he and Devlyn had plotted behind her back. The news of his illness had successfully quenched her anger and all she felt now was an immeasurable sadness.

The weather forced them to remain indoors during the next few days and Lenca spent most of the time with her grandfather. She deliberately avoided being alone with Devlyn, unable to bring herself to ask out-right the question uppermost in her mind. If he really loved her, she thought perversely, surely he would put himself out to try and win her affection, not treat her with what she could only describe as polite indifference.

Anyone would think they were casual ac-quaintances, she told herself angrily one day when he had deliberately ignored her for the best part of an hour while talking to her grandfather. Not that she wanted him to fuss, she hastened to assure herself, but it would be nice to be treated with a little more warmth. Her talk with Kip had certainly given her food for thought and she sometimes wondered whether she had been too hasty in her judgement of Devlyn.

Daniel too had refrained from mentioning their re-lationship, and she in her turn had been afraid to ques-tion him about his conspiracy as far as the *Valancia* was concerned for fear of exciting him too much.

It was her grandfather himself who brought the sub-ject up when Lenca one morning read the newspaper to him. It was very rare he did not rise as early as the rest of the household, but on this particular occasion he had expressed a desire to stay in bed.

'How's your diving going, my girl? Haven't heard

you mention it since I came home.'

'I was afraid to talk about it in case you shouted at me again,' smiled Lenca.

'Me – shout?' he said, trying to look offended. 'Only when you do something silly, like diving on your own. Now you've got Devlyn to look after you, you'll be all right. Fine fellow he is.'

Lenca winced. How many times had he told her that already? If he said it once more she would scream!

'He took me down with them the other day,' she said quickly before he could extoll Devlyn's virtues any further. 'It was very exciting. Devlyn found the missing part of the *Leeuw*'s bell.'

'Ah, yes, he told me something about that. Said you brought them luck and that he had made you a member of his team.'

'That's right. Though we haven't had a chance to dive since. I hope the weather hasn't broken altogether.'

'Don't think so, it's too early. We'll have another fine spell shortly.' He looked at Lenca keenly. 'You and Devlyn – I note you don't have much to say to each other these days. I thought you might have patched things up. Can't think why you don't like him.'

Lenca smiled sadly. 'You think the world of him, don't you, Grandfather? I'm sorry I don't share your illusions.'

Daniel sighed and pulled himself higher in the bed, clearing his throat as though about to make a speech. 'Remember the day I told you about the Trevelyan Emerald? What I didn't mention was that I'd asked Devlyn to try and find it. That's how much I trust him. There's many a person who, if they found anything of such value, would be away without a word. But I know I can rely on Devlyn.'

'But it could never be yours, Grandfather.' Lenca was

relieved he had told her himself and felt it advisable not to tell him that Devlyn had already confessed.

'I know, child, that's the sad part. But even to see it would be an experience.' His eyes closed as he allowed his mind to dwell on the possibility of possessing the Trevelyan Emerald, even for a few short hours. 'I'm an old man now. It would make me very happy to see it before—'

'Grandfather, don't!' cried Lenca, kneeling beside the bed and taking his lined old hand in hers. 'Please don't.'

He looked at her and smiled. 'You're a good child. When Devlyn told me he'd asked you to marry him I could almost see my dreams coming true. I was very sad when you turned him down.'

Lenca lowered her eyes, suddenly unable to face him. She felt – almost ashamed, almost as though she had done him an injustice. If only she could voice her suspicions – but he wouldn't believe her. No one would. It was a disappointment she had to bear alone.

He spoke again, faintly now as if tired. 'Why not bury that stubborn pride and admit that you love him? It would give me great pleasure.'

'But—'

'Don't deny it, Helenca. I'm not such an old fool that I can't see what's going on in my own house.'

'You're right, Grandfather.' Lenca looked into the misty grey eyes. 'I do love him, though I refuse to admit it, even to myself.'

'But why? What have you got against him?'

'I – I thought he was trying to swindle you. I suspected he was diving after the *Valancia* treasure and I – well, you never said you'd—' And I still think he wants to marry me for a share in my inheritance, she wanted to add.

'So you turned him down for my sake?' The old man's eyes filled with tears, moving Lenca far more than words. 'I love you very much, Helenca. You do the Trevelyan family credit. I'm glad I told you, because now there's nothing to stop you marrying him.'

Nothing you know about, thought Lenca, but how could she put her doubts into words? If she tackled Devlyn he would almost certainly deny it – and her grandfather, if she told him, he would laugh in her face.

'Well, is there?' Daniel shook her hand impatiently.

'I – I suppose not,' reluctantly Lenca looked at him.

'So why the hesitation? If I was in your shoes I'd be off right now to find him. What is it? Are you suddenly shy?'

There appeared no way out without hurting his feelings, and she couldn't do that – not now. The only solution would be to agree to marry Devlyn. She could insist on a long engagement and then, later, break it off. If her deception succeeded in making her grandfather happy for the rest of the time he had left it would be worth it. Devlyn's feelings did not count at this stage, nor her own. It was Daniel Trevelyan who mattered.

'It will be difficult to – to tell him – that I've changed my mind,' Lenca said at length. 'I made it perfectly plain that I distrusted him.'

'Leave it to me,' Daniel smiled. 'I'll put things right for you.'

'Oh no, you can't. I – I mean, I'd rather tell him myself.' It wouldn't do at all for her grandfather to discuss the matter with Devlyn.

Daniel looked surprised at this outburst. 'Very well, you know best.'

'I – I shall wait until an opportune moment. When

he's in a receptive mood.'

Daniel smiled. 'Give him a tot of my whisky. That should do the trick.'

Lenca nodded, her mind already moving ahead, planning how best to broach the subject. It would not be easy. They had spent so little time together recently that if she suddenly approached him and said she'd changed her mind he would be immediately suspicious. He might even guess that Daniel had had something to do with it. In fact – a possibility she had not thought about until now – he might have reversed his decision himself. This did not entirely make sense with her preconceived opinion of him, but it was worth bearing in mind before she actually committed herself. She did not want to be made feel a complete fool.

CHAPTER NINE

As Lenca had feared it was not an easy matter to bring up the subject of marriage. To all outward appearances Devlyn had accepted her refusal to have anything to do with him and it was more difficult than she had anticipated to hold even a friendly conversation. In her anxiety to please her grandfather Lenca was prepared to forget for a while her distrust of this man, but when they did speak he gave the impression of being in a hurry to escape. She felt rebuffed and hurt, even though the whole affair was of her own making. Still she refused to allow Daniel to speak to Devlyn on her behalf. This was her own problem and one she wanted to tackle herself.

Two evenings later, after a lively discussion regarding the artefacts so far found belonging to the *Leeuw*, Daniel agreed to go down the cellar and take a look. Kip, Alan and Trevor all trailed out of the room, but when Devlyn attempted to follow Daniel said, 'No, don't bother. Stay and keep Lenca company. We shan't be long.'

'If you insist,' replied Devlyn uncertainly, 'but watch those steps. They're very steep,' and he turned back into the room. Lenca was just in time to see her grandfather close one eye in an enormous wink, and knew that he had planned this to give her the opportunity she needed.

Her heartbeats accelerated rapidly at the thought of what lay ahead. She need not have worried. Devlyn himself unwittingly gave her the opening she needed.

He sat in an armchair opposite her own. A crisp

white shirt accentuated his tan and the glow from the amber shades made his eyes appear almost black. Lenca looked away quickly as her eyes met his. It was becoming all too easy to forget her doubts and mistrust. Each time they met her heart skipped a beat and she was afraid of giving herself away. It would help in the role she was going to play, there was no doubt of that, but she must watch her step.. There could never be any question of marriage. No matter how deeply she loved him she was not prepared to take for a husband a man whose ultimate goal was the financial rewards to be gained by such a union. Wedlock so far as Lenca was concerned was not to be treated lightly. Both partners should be prepared to give themselves utterly and wholly one to the other. Wealth should not enter into the arrangement. She knew her love for Devlyn would not fade whether he was a pauper or a king – if only he could feel the same way about her . . .

'You've been very preoccupied these last few days.' Devlyn's voice penetrated her thoughts. 'I'm beginning to wonder whether it was wise telling you about Daniel. He's sure to notice there's something wrong.'

'It – it's not that.' Lenca was thankful for the subdued light which hid her blushes. This was her moment, so why the sudden lump in her throat? She swallowed. 'I – I—' The words just would not come. 'I've given a good deal of thought to – to what you said the other day. I – realize now how I've misjudged you.' Oh God, it was difficult. Why didn't he help instead of just sitting there waiting? A word of encouragement was all she needed. 'I – I'm sorry, Devlyn.'

'I see.'

Was that *all* he could say? If only he would smile instead of looking at her with that enigmatic gleam in his eyes.

'I – I'd like to be friends again.'

His brows lifted imperceptibly. 'I didn't realize we were not friends.'

Lenca looked down at her hands, unconsciously twisting the gold ring that had belonged to her mother. 'You know what I mean,' she said quietly. She couldn't swallow her pride altogether. A line had to be drawn somewhere.

And then he was kneeling beside her. A firm finger lifted her chin so that she was forced to face him. Her eyes were bright with unshed tears and when she saw the tenderness in his eyes she heard herself say, 'I love you,' wondering instantly whether she had gone mad. She hadn't meant to say that. Not ever. It had been the last thing in her mind. Hot shame stung her cheeks, and then suddenly it didn't matter. She was being pulled to her feet, Devlyn's arms were about her, crushing her inexorably to him. Her lips parted beneath his own and for a space all else was forgotten. She was suspended in a star-spangled world of darkness – a world of ecstasy, a world of desire. Her response was overwhelming; she seemed unable to stop herself. It was not until he dragged his lips away from hers that harsh reality made her struggle free. She had never intended to go this far. She had planned their relationship on a light and friendly nature, with maybe a kiss or two thrown in for good measure. Certain that Devlyn had no real love for her, she had never suspected he would react so strongly to her plea for friendship.

'Have I alarmed you, my darling? I'm sorry.' He stroked her hair gently until Lenca felt herself relax. 'It's all so wonderful I can hardly believe it's true.' His eyes searched her face eagerly. 'I won't ask any questions now, I'm only too thankful that you've changed your mind. Oh, wait until Daniel finds out! You – you will marry me?'

To Lenca he sounded a little too eager, and although it reaffirmed her suspicions she felt a sharp stab of disappointment. She had subconsciously hoped that things might turn out differently. To discover that he did indeed truly love her – for herself alone – would have been the culmination of all her desires. Instead she was forced to accept the dismal truth that he was still after her inheritance. There was nothing she could do about it. She had more or less promised her grandfather that she would marry Devlyn, so for the time being she must go ahead with this farce – for that was all it was. She was in love with a man whose only love was avarice. So long as she did not forget this; so long as she did not allow her heart to rule her head, all would be well.

She nodded, unable to bring herself to utter the lie which constituted her assent, closing her eyes to the gleam of – was it triumph? – she saw cross his face.

Once more his lips were against hers. All resistance melted as she experienced the thrill of pleasure his nearness gave. Unable to help herself, she returned kiss for kiss, his passion deepening as he felt her response. When at last he raised his head she felt weak and defenceless, and not a little afraid of her own emotions.

'We'll tell your grandfather when he returns,' said Devlyn softly, 'and tomorrow we'll make plans.'

'So soon?' protested Lenca, feeling herself being washed along on a tide too strong to resist. 'I – I thought we might wait a while. I'm not yet used to the idea of – of becoming your wife.'

'If you insist,' he murmured, his lips caressing her hair, 'but not too long.'

She was still in his arms when Daniel and the other

men came back into the room. Her grandfather's smile of satisfaction when he saw them together more than rewarded Lenca for the guilt she felt. At least she had made one person happy. Two, if Devlyn was included, even though his happiness was destined for a short life.

'Looks as if congratulations are in order,' said Daniel, looking from one to the other.

'Indeed they are,' beamed Devlyn, pulling Lenca close into the circle of his arm. 'Don't you think I'm lucky?'

'Thought you'd never get round to it,' grumbled Daniel, kissing Lenca and shaking the younger man by the hand.

'You've your granddaughter to blame for that. Took her long enough to make up her mind!'

Daniel gave Lenca a fond smile. 'I suppose she wanted to be sure. This calls for drinks all round. Go and tell Meg to bring a bottle of champagne.'

Congratulations flowed as freely as the wine until Lenca felt the whole evening had taken on an air of unreality. Kip had been genuine in his wishes for her future happiness, and Lenca knew he felt that their earlier conversation had been instrumental in bringing about her engagement. She would like to tell him the truth, but of course this was impossible. If her grandfather had the merest suspicion that she knew of his illness he would never forgive Devlyn for telling her.

On several occasions during the evening Lenca noticed how tired her grandfather looked, though when she suggested he go to bed he immediately told her not to fuss. It was no surprise, therefore, when the next morning Meg told Lenca not to disturb her master as he was still sleeping.

In the dining room Devlyn greeted her with a brilliant smile and a kiss, watched with tolerant amusement by his three friends. 'And how's my beautiful Lenca this morning?'

Lenca, who had woken with the feeling that last night had all been a dream, replied, 'All right – I think. I still feel a bit – bemused.'

'That's what being engaged to me does. You'll never be the same again, I assure you.'

'There's promises,' jested Alan.

'No, I think it was the champagne,' Lenca smiled. 'I did drink rather a lot.'

'Now she's gone and demoralized me,' rejoined Devlyn to no one in particular. 'How like a woman!'

All through breakfast Devlyn kept up this light-hearted, affectionate teasing, and Lenca wondered why he couldn't always be like this. It was infinitely preferable to his dark moods and the fatherly air he had adopted of late. She found herself responding gladly and when he suggested a ride into Falmouth to choose her engagement ring she laughingly agreed before remembering that theirs was an engagement with a difference. There would never be any marriage, so what was the point of a ring? There was no way out, though. He mustn't discover the truth until she found it necessary to tell him – and meantime she was to all outward appearances his fiancée, so a ring she must wear.

'If the weather had been good enough we'd have gone diving today instead,' remarked Devlyn as they set out on their journey.

'So you put your work before me?' she replied lightly.

'Do I hell?' with a look that made Lenca's pulses race. 'But you know what the weather's like. I have to take every chance I get.'

'I know. I wouldn't really have minded. In fact I'm

173

looking forward to our next dive.'

'What do you hope to find? The Trevelyan Emerald?' He spoke easily, but Lenca knew how important this find would be to him.

'But of course. Isn't that what we're both after?'

She thought he gave her a funny look, but he said no more about it. Instead he asked the question Lenca had been expecting.

'What made you change your mind so suddenly about me? I'm not complaining, just curious.'

'I thought you knew.' She slanted him a quick glance, but his eyes were on the road ahead. The lanes were so narrow that they took all his attention. 'I – I suspected you of trying to defraud Grandfather, but—' with a slight shrug, 'now I know you were searching at his own request.'

'How could I have cheated him? We both know the terms of the will. My reward would have been entirely self-satisfaction.'

'I know that – now,' said Lenca uncomfortably. 'That's why I – apologized.'

He smiled then. 'I'm glad you did. I couldn't have stood your suspicions much longer.'

'I didn't know it bothered you. You certainly gave the impression of being very unconcerned.'

'Men don't show their feelings as much as women – you should know that.'

There was silence for a while as he negotiated some particularly tricky bends and then as their lane joined the main road into Falmouth he spoke again:

'You still don't quite trust me, do you, Lenca?'

She shot him a startled glance. 'What do you mean?' Surely she had given every impression of being a completely devoted fiancée? It hadn't been difficult, loving him as she did.

'I'm not quite sure what I do mean,' he said. 'But once or twice last night I felt that you were holding something back.'

How he had formed these suspicions Lenca could not imagine. She had thought herself that her performance was pretty good. So far as she could recall she had given him no reason to doubt her love. Whatever it was he had noticed proved one thing – she must be extra careful in future unless she wanted to disrupt her grandfather's happiness. He had little enough to look forward to without Lenca adding to his problems.

'You're imagining things,' she said, purposely injecting a note of humour into her voice and placing a slightly unsteady hand on his arm. 'I love you, Devlyn. Isn't that enough?'

He caught her fingers. 'Perhaps it's all too good to be true and I'm looking for the fly in the ointment. I'm sorry.'

But was he? Lenca watching him warily saw that he still seemed to have a great deal on his mind, though when they reached Falmouth he shook off whatever was bothering him and set out to be the most attentive of companions.

The ring Lenca would have chosen was a modest solitaire set in platinum, but Devlyn insisted she accept one with a large amethyst instead of diamonds. 'To match the colour of your eyes,' he said gently.

It was a beautiful ring and Lenca was very conscious of it on her finger as they left the shop. It had been very expensive and she was afraid she might lose it, touching it every now and then to make sure it was still there.

'Can't you believe it yet?' asked Devlyn, noting her action. 'Do you still find our engagement as much a mystery as I do?'

Lenca knew he teased, but it was so near to the truth

that she was afraid to look into his eyes. He was too perceptive by far and she would have to be very, very careful to keep up the deception.

After their shopping expedition they lunched in one of Falmouth's best restaurants, then took a leisurely round about tour back home. In view of Devlyn's earlier comments about her distrust Lenca paid far more attention to him than she had intended. Consequently it was a very elated couple who arrived at Trevelyan Manor a few hours later.

Daniel was half asleep in his favourite armchair, but woke immediately they burst in.

'You both look very happy,' he said, his face wreathed in smiles. 'It does my heart good to see you. What have you been doing with yourselves all day?'

Lenca held out her hand. 'We've been shopping.'

'Come here, child. Let me see.'

Obediently Lenca put her hand into his. Grey head bent for a few moments over the ring and when he looked up there was a suspicion of tears in his eyes. 'Thank you, Helenca,' he whispered, 'thank you.'

Lenca knew what he meant, but Devlyn? Had he heard? Would he wonder what Daniel was thanking her for? She looked round fearfully, but Devlyn was smiling. 'It looks as though she's made you as happy as she has me, Daniel. I must thank you for bringing your granddaughter to this house, otherwise we'd never have met.'

'I think some day, somewhere you would,' said the old man wisely. 'You're made for each other. When's the happy day going to be? Or haven't you made up your minds yet? I don't want to be kept waiting long.'

'Then you'd better speak to Lenca,' Devlyn advised. 'Says she doesn't want to be rushed. It would suit me if we were married tomorrow, but you know what women are like.'

Daniel snorted. 'What's this, Helenca? Why do you want to wait?'

Trapped between them, Lenca searched her mind for a feasible excuse. They both waited. Her grandfather with ill-controlled impatience and Devlyn with – an almost calculated expression which she interpreted as *Get out of that if you can*. He knows I'm stalling for time, she thought. Despite her attempts to convince him that her love was genuine he still doubted her. She crossed to his side and linked her hand through his arm, looking up into the watchful blue eyes.

'No woman likes to be rushed,' she said. 'There's so much to be arranged, so much to think about. Anyway,' in sudden inspiration, 'I've always fancied a summer wedding. No one likes to stand about shivering.'

'It's not winter yet,' grumbled her grandfather. 'You go ahead and arrange your wedding – soon. There's still some fine weather to come. You forget I'm an old man. I may not be here next year.'

How could he say such things? thought Lenca achingly. How could he joke about the inevitable? Admittedly she was not supposed to know, but it made matters no easier. With a muffled cry she dropped to her knees at his side. 'I've told you not to speak like that,' she cried.

'Who knows how long any of us have left?' He gently stroked Lenca's hair. 'What is to be will be. That's why you two young people should lose no opportunity to grasp what happiness you can, while you can. Devlyn, take no notice of this young madam. Go ahead and make your arrangements. She'll have nothing to argue about then.'

'Grandfather!'

But Daniel ignored Lenca's protest. 'The ceremony will be at St. Keverne Church, and I shall have great pleasure in leading you up the aisle myself.'

'Devlyn! Say something.' Lenca looked imploringly at her fiancé, but he too followed her grandfather's lead and affected not to hear her pleas for help. Indeed he looked highly amused by the whole situation – and pleased, Lenca noted with disgust.

'Let's see,' her grandfather was saying. 'Three weeks for the banns. Unless you want a special licence? No! A month today, then – how about that?'

'That will suit me fine, *sir*,' said Devlyn smartly. 'I'll ring the vicar right away.'

Lenca felt trapped, like a caged leopard knowing he could not escape. There was no way out without hurting Daniel, and she loved him too dearly for that. She crossed to the window, staring out at the splendour of autumn. The trees are dying, she thought, as a handful of leaves gambolled across the lawns. As too are my hopes for freedom. But theirs is a mock death, for in the spring they will live again – whereas my heart will be tied for ever to a man who doesn't love me.

'What's the matter, child?' Daniel's arm came down heavily on her shoulder. 'Aren't you happy?'

Swallowing her distress, Lenca smiled bravely. 'Of course. Why do you ask?'

'You seem – preoccupied.'

'A little confused,' she said. 'Everything's happening so quickly.'

'No sense in dilly-dallying. Life's too short for that. Why did you insist on waiting? There's not something still troubling you?'

'Oh no,' she lied, 'I just don't like rushing things, that's all.'

He shook his head. 'You're a strange young woman. Most people in love can't wait to get married.'

That's because they're sure of their feelings for one another, thought Lenca wryly. If I were certain Devlyn loved me how different things would be. As it is, what does the future hold? Marriage to a man who, once her grandfather's wealth was within his grasp, would probably want nothing more to do with her. It was a very dismal prospect, especially when things could be so different. Oh, why did I have to fall in love with him? her heart cried. Why couldn't I have carried on hating him, then there would have been no problem.

During the next few weeks Lenca felt that she was being swept along on a tide of misfortune. Meg, Daniel and Devlyn made arrangements with no thought of consulting her; they took it for granted that she was agreeable. A dressmaker was called in to take measurements for her wedding gown, caterers were booked, the whole house cleaned from top to bottom and rooms flung open that Lenca had never seen before. An air of unreality hung over all with Lenca feeling curiously detached, as though she was on the outside looking in.

She was not unhappy – Devlyn made sure of that. The hours they spent together were full of love and sunshine and pleasure. It was only when she remembered the reason behind his proposal that the future looked black. On several occasions they went diving and found many more artefacts belonging to the *Leeuw*. Lenca really enjoyed these periods in the underwater world. It was here that her worries disappeared like sunkissed snow. In the cool, green depths she was perfectly happy and content. Devlyn was her natural diving companion and no longer did he seem suspicious of her motives for wanting to dive on the Manacles. She knew it was because it made no difference now, but even this knowledge did not worry her while under the surface.

Her grandfather too showed great excitement in the forthcoming wedding, never forgetting to remind Lenca how indebted he was to her for making an old man happy.

'Anyone would think I was only marrying him to please you,' jested Lenca.

'No, child. It's easy to see you love him.'

And Lenca was glad that he should think like this.

Three days before the wedding, a day which dawned grey and dismal and which had surprisingly turned into beautiful warm autumn sunshine, Devlyn suggested one last dive before finishing for the season.

Accordingly after lunch they stowed their gear into the cars and made their way down to Porthoustock beach. The customary feeling of exhilaration whipped Lenca's senses into a frenzy of excitement and she sat on the edge of her seat as they zipped across the water, the outboard throwing back two curving plumes of foam.

Kip, Alan and Trevor went down first, with the intention of Lenca and Devlyn taking their turn afterwards. They had not gone long, however, before Kip surfaced and beckoned excitedly to Devlyn.

'Looks as if they've found something. Will you be all right?'

'Of course, don't worry.'

'I'll send one of the others back up. I don't like the idea of you being here all alone.' And with that he sat on the edge of the boat and rolled backwards into the water.

Lenca sat on in the warm sunshine, agog with curiosity and longing to find out what had caused Kip's animation. Her mind naturally turned to the *Valancia*, forgetting that the other men knew nothing about this ship. Wouldn't it be wonderful if the Trevelyan Emerald was found? Then common sense told her that he would have brought up such a small item, not fetched Devlyn down. No, it must be something big — but what? No matter how Lenca puzzled over this intriguing question she could find no answer.

Instead she allowed her mind to dwell on her forthcoming wedding. It would be a bittersweet occasion and she could not help but feel nervous about the whole affair. Everything was ready now. Her gown, which was a dream in satin and pearls, hung in the wardrobe; friends from Birmingham had been invited and were coming tomorrow to stay for a few days. Meg had shown surprising artistic talent in making the wedding cake herself. An air of feverish excitement hung over the Manor. Only Lenca had any reservations. She was afraid of what the future might hold. To be Devlyn's wife, loved and cherished as a woman should be, was a thought sweeter than wine, but she knew their marriage would never be like that and it tore her heart in two every time she thought about it.

Resolutely she pushed these disturbing thoughts to the back of her mind. No matter how deeply she would be hurt in the future she must go through with the ceremony. She owed it to her grandfather. There were times now when he looked extremely ill, though he always shrugged away any enquiries of concern. 'I'm just a bit tired,' he would say, or, 'Don't fuss. It's only a headache.' But Lenca knew, and was deeply distressed. She could not help feeling resentful that her mother had kept her away from this darling man for so many years. There was a rapport between them that came as naturally as if they were father and daughter. In fact, he was the father Lenca had never known, and she spent hours at his side recounting adventures of her childhood; Daniel listening with avid interest to every tiny detail. Although their friendship would only last a short time Lenca knew he would hold a special place in her heart for ever.

She shivered and stretched her stiff legs. It seemed as though the men had been away for hours. She knew it couldn't have been – their air wouldn't allow it – but that was what it felt like.

By now the sun was a pale face in an opaque sky. Glancing back at the once distant shoreline, Lenca could see the merest sign of fog. Involuntarily her heartbeats quickened and she willed the men to hurry up. The rocks were hazardous enough without the added danger of fog to hamper their journey back.

As she watched and waited the sea became calm, the wind dropped away to nothing, and she felt tense and uneasy. Somewhere behind the high swirling fog the sun was a ball of gold, but here on the strangely still and silent water Lenca's spirits became lower and lower.

The Manacle bell, which she had scarcely noticed on any other occasion, tolled out its gloomy warning. The seconds seemed like minutes and the minutes like hours. Lenca dragged out a blanket from the wooden locker and draped it round her shoulders to try and instil some warmth into her frozen limbs. All she wore was a wet suit over her bikini and as the impending fog suddenly dropped like a thick curtain so too it became even colder.

'Oh, please hurry!' she called, startled by the sound of her own voice in this eerie silence.

It was then that she felt herself drifting.

Stifling the panic that rose in her throat, Lenca

pulled on the anchor rope. As she had half expected the end came away in her hand, its frayed edges indicating the cutting power of an unseen portion of the Manacles. She had been warned of this eventuality — but for it to happen now . . .

She closed her eyes for a second. 'Oh, God, what am I to do?' Trembling in every limb, she cowered down on her seat, expecting every moment to feel the crunch of splintering wood as the boat's keel caught on one of the perilous rocks. Afraid to use the engine, or the oars, she paddled softly with her fingers, trying to stop herself drifting too far away from her original position.

If Devlyn and his friends surfaced and there was no boat waiting — what would they do? It didn't bear thinking about. She was afraid, more afraid than she had ever been in her whole life. Four lives depended on her. She must keep calm, fight the near-hysteria that welled up inside. 'Devlyn!' she called, 'Kip! I'm over here.' But no answering voices called from the mist. Repeatedly she shouted their names, hearing her own voice echo mockingly back, but no reassuring reply. 'Why are they taking so long? What is it they've found?' She spoke half aloud, feeling the need for some sound in this noiseless, muffled world, even if it was only her own voice.

As the fog drifted the sun appeared intermittently like a red, smoking ball, but none of its heat reached through the swirling mist. It was low in the sky. Soon it would be dark. Tears mingled with the damp on Lenca's face. She did not relish the prospect of spending the night at sea.

Soon after that she noticed that the rocks around her had taken on a different shape. She had lost all sense of direction. Goodness knows how far she had floated from Pen-win Rock. 'Devlyn!' she cried, her voice now shrill with anguish. 'Devlyn! Where are you?'

Silence! Frightening, threatening silence, broken only by the tolling bell.

And then, faintly at first but getting nearer all the time, the throb of an engine and the distant wail of a foghorn.

Lenca cupped her hands round her mouth. 'Help!' and 'Help-help!' echoed back out of the mist. She called again and again, but to no avail. She could hear the boat's engines ticking over. They were searching – why couldn't they hear her? *'Over here!'* she called, and then as the fog thinned for a vital second she saw the wraithlike outline of a trawler. The setting sun behind her made an unforgettable picture as she slid through the mist, but as suddenly as she appeared she was gone.

No matter. Now that Lenca knew help was at hand her spirits rose. In case they had not seen her she started the engine. Now they would know in which direction to search.

The fog thickened and a voice surprisingly near hailed, 'Ahoy there!'

'Hello – o!' called back Lenca, peering through the gloom trying to make out the shape of the ship.

'We can't come any nearer. Try and follow us.'

She inched the boat forward, following the sound of their foghorn. Suddenly a line of grey, shadowy rocks crossed her course and she swung hard over to starboard. They towered above her in mysterious shrouded shapes. In the gloom she had lost all sense of proportion and when she saw a row of gigantic birds, as still and silent as statues, her heart gave a sudden lurch, before she realized that they were only seagulls.

Concentrating on steering clear of the rocks, Lenca did not notice that the sound of the trawler was fading, until suddenly she stopped and listened. Somehow they had become separated. She could hear voices, but faintly – and they were receding! The sun had set. It would soon be dark. She burst into muffled sobs.

And then remembrance of Devlyn and the others pulled her up short. At least she had the boat. They were probably somewhere out there on the surface, bobbing about in the freezing water, searching for her and wondering what had happened. And Grandfather – what would he be thinking? Would he guess that they were stranded out in the foggy English Channel, or would he presume they had headed for shore at the first signs of mist and were waiting in safety for it to clear?

Gingerly she edged forward. Anything was better than sitting waiting, not knowing how long it would be before she was found. Suddenly the wail of the trawler's siren sounded again. Lenca headed in the direction of the horn. It seemed like hours that she trailed the wailing siren, dodging rocks, turning and doubling back. At times feeling almost like giving up in her despair.

It was a bitter world in which she had been so abruptly plunged, an icy world of moisture. The blanket had long since fallen from her shoulders, sodden and useless. The dank dew washed her hair, her suit gleamed like polished jet. Frigid beads of water stuck to her eyelashes and eyebrows and hung in stone-cold droplets from her chin and nose.

Without realizing it Lenca all at once found she had steered clear of the rocks and was now in the open sea. She breathed easier as the trawler sounded close at hand and in the density of the fog almost collided before discovering it was right beside her.

Willing hands reached down and strong arms pulled her aboard. So great was her relief that she clung gratefully to the figure of her rescuer. It was not until he spoke that Lenca became aware of his identity.

'Lenca, my own sweet love, I think I'd have killed myself had anything happened to you!' Devlyn's anguished voice penetrated her stupor and in that moment Lenca knew that he loved her. It was no game. His affection was genuine. One look at his tormented face told her so. No one could look like that and not mean it.

Regardless of the curious eyes of the ship's crew, and the amusement shown by Kip and his friends, she tilted her face and met his lips in a mutually satisfying kiss which told them both what they wanted to know. It had taken near-tragedy to bring her to her senses. But now she knew as confidently as though he had said it. Devlyn loved her!

There was no time for conversation. All eyes were needed to guide them back to shore. It was a long and tiring journey, but they eventually reached the safety of Porthoustock beach. The skipper was thanked for his trouble and they piled into the cars for the last leg of this incredible journey.

Daniel hovered impatiently in the hall.

'Thank goodness you're back!' he breathed. 'I've been half out of my mind with worry. What happened? Why didn't you return at the first sign of fog?'

'We had no idea,' confessed Devlyn, 'until we surfaced. By then it was thick. If it hadn't been for the trawler passing we might have still been out there.'

'What do you mean?' frowned Daniel. 'It shouldn't have been too difficult to find your way back.'

'We lost the boat,' said Devlyn simply.

'You left it unattended?' Sceptical tones sharpened Daniel's voice.

'Oh no, Lenca was in it, but—'

'The anchor line broke,' interrupted Lenca. 'We got separated.'

Daniel's eyes narrowed. 'I'm surprised at you leaving Lenca like that.'

Devlyn grimaced. 'I'm sorry, but something important cropped up. Wait until I tell you wh—'

'More important than my granddaughter's life?' Daniel growled ferociously. 'I'll have more to say about this. Meantime I think you'd all better have hot baths before you catch pneumonia.'

Lenca kissed her grandfather's cheek and skipped upstairs ahead of the men. Daniel would have simmered down by the time they had washed and changed. She herself was undaunted by his attitude. Her discovery regarding the true state of Devlyn's feelings had left her in a state of euphoria. How could she have been so blind? He loved her. He loved her! She felt like shouting it from the rooftops.

Hurriedly she bathed and dressed, eager to be alone with Devlyn, to feel again the strength of his love as he swept her into his arms. He must have had the same idea, for he appeared at her door just as she was about to leave.

'Lenca,' he murmured, pushing her back into the room and closing the door behind him. 'Lenca, can you ever forgive me?'

Her heart beat wildly as she looked at the lean strength of him, at the blond curls clinging damply to his well-shaped head, the blue eyes infinitely tender as he took her into his arms.

'There's nothing to forgive,' she whispered. 'It wasn't your fault.'

'I should never have left you – your grandfather was right.'

'We're safe now, that's all that matters,' and she lifted

her face and kissed him gently.

'You're very sweet,' he said, 'and different too. What's happened?'

Lenca shook her head and smiled mysteriously, burying her face against the soft silk of his shirt. 'I love you, Devlyn.'

'And I love you.'

'Do you really?' She looked at him swiftly, anxiously. 'Do you *really* love me, Devlyn?'

'But of course I do, you silly, sweet idiot. What makes you ask?'

'I wanted to be sure.'

His kiss was gentle yet firm, full of unleashed passion, and left Lenca hungering for more.

'Does that help?' His eyes gently mocked her.

'Yes.' The word escaped shyly from her lips before she pulled away and turned her back on him. 'I – I have a confession to make.' She must tell him. She could not start married life with this feeling of guilt for ever in the background.

He was close behind her now, his hands on her shoulders, his breath warm against the back of her neck. Lenca trembled at his touch. 'I – I thought you w-wanted to marry me for – for all this,' indicating the house and garden with a sweeping movement of her arm. 'I thought—'

His finger touched her lips, stemming further words. 'So that's it! You've a fertile imagination, young Lenca. You must learn to control it.' He twisted her round to face him. 'First you think I'm trying to swindle Daniel and then when that doesn't succeed you think I want to marry you as another means of getting my hands on his money. Let me tell you, I'd love you if you had nothing – if you were a beggar girl crawling in the gutter I would still love you. I half guessed this was on your mind – but if so why did you agree to marry me? You have me baffled.'

Delicate colour suffused Lenca's cheeks and she lowered her lashes to hide the shame his open words had caused.

'Grandfather wanted me to. I did it to make him happy.'

His eyes glittered. 'Yet you professed to love me. I'm beginning to wonder which is truth and which is fiction.'

'I did – I do. I couldn't help myself, even though I doubted your intentions.'

He tilted her chin and she looked at him.

'That makes you all the more worthy of my love,' he said softly, kissing the tip of her upturned nose.

'He must never find out I suspected your motives,' her voice anxious now. 'He knows I love you. He had no idea.'

'It shall be our secret. I too love your grandfather. We must do all we can to make him happy.'

Silence filled the room as their lips met in an eminently satisfying kiss. Silence save for the thudding of two hearts as one.

'Devlyn,' said Lenca several minutes later, 'what *was* it that kept you down so long this afternoon?'

His eyes glinted wickedly. 'Nothing much – just a chestful of treasure, that's all.'

Harlequin Reader Service

ORDER FORM

MAIL COUPON TO

Harlequin Reader Service,
M.P.O. Box 707,
Niagara Falls, New York 14302.

Canadian **SEND**
Residents **TO:**

Harlequin Reader Service
Stratford, Ont. N5A 6W4

Please check Volumes requested.

☐ 1	☐ 2	☐ 3	☐ 4	☐ 5
☐ 7	☐ 8	☐ 9	☐ 10	☐ 11
☐ 12	☐ 13	☐ 14	☐ 15	☐ 16
☐ 17	☐ 18	☐ 19	☐ 20	☐ 21
☐ 22	☐ 23	☐ 24	☐ 25	☐ 26
☐ 27	☐ 28	☐ 29	☐ 30	☐ 31
☐ 32	☐ 33	☐ 34	☐ 35	☐ 36
☐ 37				

Please send me by return mail the books which I have checked.
I am enclosing 95¢ for each book ordered

Number of books ordered _____ @ 95¢ each = $ _____

Postage and Handling = .25

TOTAL = $ _____

Name _____

Address _____

City _____

State/Prov. _____

Zip/Postal Code _____

information please

**All the Exciting News from
Under the Harlequin Sun**

It costs you nothing to receive our news bulletins and
intriguing brochures. From our brand new releases to our
money-saving 3-in-1 omnibus and valuable best-selling
back titles, our information package is sure to be a hit.
Don't miss out on any of the exciting details. Send for
your Harlequin INFORMATION PLEASE package today.